FAKE FIANCÉ

AMY MCKINLEY

ARROWSCOPE PRESS, LLC

Fake Fiancé

(p) **ISBN-13**: 978-1-951919-85-6

(e) **ISBN-13**: 978-1-951919-83-2

Publisher: Arrowscope Press, LLC; www.arrowscopepress.com

Editing—Taylor Anhalt

Cover Design—T.E. Black Designs; www.teblackdesigns.com

Author photo provided by—Brookelyn Anhalt of lovely.life.photography; https://www.facebook.com/LovelyLifePhotography-102253596490708

Interior Formatting & Design— Arrowscope Press, LLC; www.arrowscopepress.com

CHAPTER 1

ADELINE

$\mathcal{A}$ sense of heaviness hung in the air as I sat at the small folding table my best friend Eileen had set up for the psychic. I waited in silence across from her, shifting in my chair, unsure what to do as this was my first time meeting, let alone talking to, a medium. We'd already exchanged hellos, and I wasn't about to offer up any details about who I was. Instead, I passed the awkwardness by studying the woman before me.

Long waves of black hair surrounded a face of indiscernible age. I couldn't pinpoint it—twenty-eight, thirty-five, or older? Small laugh lines framed eyes and mouth set in an olive-toned face that maintained a youthful quality, but her eyes—those were ancient.

Downstairs, the sound of music and laughter from the small party in our sorority house carried on. That was where I wanted to be—enjoying the excitement of a carefree night with my friends, celebrating all we've accomplished. Instead I was upstairs sitting across from a woman I didn't know, who was supposed to connect me to people who had passed. I fought the urge to twist a lock of my hair and instead twined my fingers in my lap. I didn't know why I was so nervous.

It was supposed to be fun.

Chills ran up and down my spine as she leaned forward, her bracelets clinking. Mysterious obsidian eyes reflected something otherworldly that I couldn't define or understand. I wanted to rub my arms but clasped my hands tight instead. Electricity charged the air, and all the fine hairs on my body stood on end.

I wasn't having fun.

Seconds ticked by, then on an inhaled breath, she slowly blinked, a soft smile curving her full red lips upward. "Adeline, interesting name." Her gaze turned introspective. "Your mother is with us."

I fought the urge to stand up and walk away. But the fact that she knew something about my mom kept me in my seat. I craved hearing anything about her, even if this entire thing wasn't real. I missed her terribly.

"She says she named you appropriately. Someone in your family tree had the name Adeline, but she died… at sea." Her eyes remained unfocused, and she tilted her head as if listening to someone whisper in her ear.

"I don't understand what you're saying. I'm supposed to die at sea?" As I waited for her answer, I shifted in my chair, unsure what to think. Mom had been into our family history before she passed, but I wasn't. I barely remembered who that person was that shared my name. I'd thought Mom just liked it.

"No, nothing like that. Your mother says she's proud of you."

I jumped as the psychic's voice pierced my thoughts of Mom. *Proud of me.* That was something I knew, and it was rather generic. My skepticism returned in full.

Mom died years ago from cancer, leaving my father and

me to figure out our suddenly strained relationship. Not going to lie and say it was easy—it was anything but. Promises were made before Dad, too, passed away.

A soft smile curved the psychic's face. "She says she has no regrets."

Maybe. My parents were happy, blissfully so, despite the hard times, lack of money, and failing business. "But you gave up being a model when you met Dad. You were on a path for success." I couldn't help it. I spoke as if Mom could hear me. I wanted to believe she could.

"She says, 'That wasn't the life I wanted. I wanted a family. There wasn't a day that I regretted marrying the love of my life. But you, my darling daughter, have a different path. Follow it and find your happy.'"

Even said in the medium's voice, that would have been something my mom would have said. Chills danced along my bare arms, and I wished I'd worn something over my thread-bare "I run because I really like beer" T-shirt. Emotions were too close to the surface, and tonight I didn't want to succumb to them. I was starting out on a new adventure, and so were my friends. Mom was right, even though leaving was bitter-sweet, I wanted to "find my happy." I didn't feel as if it was here.

Relaxing back, I decided not to take myself seriously. The experience should be at least interesting, even if I weren't having a great time. I gave the woman a slight nod. And really, I wasn't positive I believed in what she was saying, part of me thought it could be my deep desire to connect to my mom, to hear her words and feel her presence, even if only for a few minutes.

The rational side of my brain rejected that this woman could actually connect with the dead. As for the medium knowing my name, Eileen must have told her, no big deal.

She could've researched all of us at the party on the internet and learned that my mom died.

"She's insisting you follow your heart, that you need to leave the area."

"Why?" I couldn't resist. I'd planned to skip town on the heels of my college graduation, which was tomorrow. There wasn't anything holding me here. Not Tommy, that was for sure—despite the plans he had for us.

The woman tilted her head, her gaze once again turning inward, and a faraway look eased the lines in her face, taking years off her thirty-something appearance. "The neighbor isn't the one. She says your father is with her and regrets pushing you. She's pointing to…" Her eyes sharpened, and my back snapped straight. "You're a designer? No, that's not what she meant. There's an inn and a man that owns it. You're to go there."

"I'm flying out the morning after graduation. Did Eileen tell you this?" My voice held an edge of skepticism I couldn't hide. Business tycoon Stone Crenshaw recently bought a hotel in Italy, expanding his New York-based business to Europe, and I'd applied for the position of executive assistant. With my multiple summer jobs, helping my dad on the office end of his construction company, business degree and internship experience through another of Stone's hotels, I was qualified. And apparently, he was desperate.

Thanks to my sorority connections, I was able to get pushed to the top of the application list and recommended by his current assistant, and sorority alumna. Again, the psychic could have heard about this from anyone in my sorority.

The medium smiled and tapped the table with a long copper-painted nail. "You will have success there, in time." She tilted her head to the left—her go-to move before she dropped something weird on me—her dark eyes narrowed, and the smile fell away. "Wait."

A frown deepened the grooves around her mouth, and my heart skipped a beat. I toyed with the Saint Valentine pendant worn on a silver chain around my neck. The "in time" comment about my success concerned me a little. Obstacles weren't unusual, but I was determined. I would change my lot in life. I would not be destitute like my parents or trapped as my mother was to a man she loved so much she gave up her budding career. She'd always said she didn't regret it, but I think a part of her had. Why couldn't she have had both the man she loved as well as a career?

"There is another here." The room chilled. "So insistent."

I swore the air crackled with electricity while phantom fingertips danced along my arms, and I shivered.

She shook her head. "Hmm. He's agitated. I can't quite understand him. But this name, it's important. Cristiano Santoro." Her brows scrunched, and she leaned forward slightly. "Oh… your mom is back. She's adamant that you look him up."

A wave of sadness washed over me, the likes of which I hadn't felt since we buried my mom. That name. Tears formed and rolled in rapid succession down my cheeks. *Dammit.* Either his name had triggered me or the continued talk about my mom as if the medium actually saw her.

I swiped the wetness from my face and shoved the unwanted and unexplained feelings aside as best as I could. Strangest few minutes of my life. The pressure in the room eased. Another of my sisters noisily came up the stairs and leaned against the doorjamb. The medium flashed me a smile before her focus shifted away from me. I thanked her and slipped past Monica, my sorority sister, who was anxious for her turn.

I made my way back to the main room and shed the odd

sense of déjà vu, welcoming the rather loud music that poured from the stereo in the corner. Josie handed me a drink as I stepped off the last stair. I spotted Eileen near the back wall, sitting on the couch with Lauren. When Eileen saw me, a shriek shattered the last of my tension before she launched herself off the cushions at me.

Laughing, I returned her hug before she pulled back, squeezing my shoulders. "So? How was it? What did she say?"

I plastered a smile on my face, determined not to ruin this for her. She'd set it up with me in mind, even though it was an event for all our sisters. She knew I was missing Mom so much more after Dad passed six months ago. It'd been a tough semester. "It was…" I couldn't help it. I had to know. "Did you tell her about my mom? Or that I was leaving after graduation?" Not everyone knew, and I'd thought Eileen had kept that information to herself. I was supposed to share my news about the job with them tonight, after the psychic finished. Maybe Eileen had told one of the other girls in the house.

"Nothing. She knows the first name of each one of us like what's on the sign-up sheet, and that's it." Her brows furrowed, and her fingers tightened on my shoulders as worry pulled her features taut. "I haven't told anyone that you're leaving the day after tomorrow."

"Maybe it was Tiffany then." That was the name of the alum sorority sister I'd contacted about the job. She was a few years older than us, had graduated four years ago, and worked in the position that I'd be taking over for Stone Crenshaw.

Eileen shrugged. "Maybe? But I don't think so. Everyone here wants the time to be about them. I don't think they're even thinking about what you'll be doing next." Her mouth compressed in a thin line. "Why? Did she tell you something about your new job?"

"Sort of." Pulling out my phone, I typed the name she'd given me into my notes app to check out later. "Not much. My destiny is supposed to be there, whatever that means."

"Ohh, what if you meet the man of your dreams? I mean, it is the city of love." A hopeless romantic, Eileen flashed me a wide grin while her shoulders shook in silent laughter. She knew I didn't share her fairy-tale views. "Maybe you'll find your very own Romeo in Verona—the place where Romeo and Juliet were."

"Shut your mouth. And their relationship ended in tragedy. I would have to be crazy to wish for that. Besides, you know my goal is a career. No man will distract me from achieving that."

She rolled her eyes. "Not what I meant. I wasn't referring to Tommy, but a real romance, minus the tragedy. You don't need a linebacker hinging his football success on you being present at his games. You did break it off with him, right?"

I bit my lip thinking about the best way to answer her. "Yes. I told him the other day."

Eileen narrowed her eyes. "How did you tell him?"

Crap. "In text."

"You can't be serious."

"What did you expect me to do? He never listens to me when I tell him I don't want to be together. I gave him back the ring, and this way it's in writing. He can revisit what I'd said. Besides, I'll be gone soon. It'll all work out."

"If you say so." Eileen shrugged. "Back to Italy and your prospects there. What I'm not talking about is Romeo and Juliet—but the fact that you'll be working alongside a gorgeous man." She nudged my shoulder. "And with this to-die-for, long silvery-blond hair, those eyes, and your rack…" Her finger circled the air between us and wiggled to include all of me. "Well the whole drop-dead package, he won't know what hit him." She glanced at my gym shoe-clad feet. "We better have you practice walking in heels."

I snorted at her absurd description and worked to shake off the cloak of anger that'd settled around me at the mention of my looks and meeting a man. Just the idea of using my appearance at the new job to land a husband reminded me too much of my father's outdated opinion and Tommy's pressure to get married before the NFL draft. We weren't even dating anymore. It wasn't real. I sighed, regret heavy in the knowledge that Tommy had followed me around like a puppy for our entire high school experience, then college, in a relentless pursuit.

We'd dated, sure, but I wasn't all that serious about taking the relationship any further than having fun at college. There was something missing. That spark I'd expected to feel and I know he hadn't experienced it either. And then later, when Dad fell ill… I'd only pretended Tommy and I were solid to my dad so he didn't leave this world worrying about me. But the truth was, I didn't need someone to take care of me. I'd been doing that ever since Mom died five years ago. Tommy had other ideas about that, and when he'd dropped to a knee beside Dad's hospital bed, I couldn't steal the pure joy that lit up Dad's gray features. Outside the hospital room, I'd set Tommy straight. I wasn't marrying him.

As to my looks? Eileen was high. Even though I sort of understood her point. I was young, and people were weird. But I wasn't anything special. Average. With my hair secured in a bun and professional clothes, no one would spare me a second glance. College was a cesspool of horny guys. It would be different in a business environment. I was sure of it. As for the heels comment, she may be on to something there. I never wore them.

"Let's get a drink." Distracting Eileen from her happily-ever-after fantasies would be easy with the mention of partying together.

She bounced on her toes, her curls mimicking each movement. "Yes! I'm so glad you decided to hang with us one last time before you go."

I rolled my eyes. "So much drama."

Eileen linked our elbows as we made our way over to the bottles of beer and wine. "You love that about me."

Debatable. But I would do just about anything for her. I shook off any lingering negative thoughts. Tonight wasn't for dwelling on the baggage I carried with me. I would leave it behind when I boarded my flight at the crack of dawn the day after we graduated, heading toward the future I wanted for myself. This time was about having fun with my best friend and sisters. They mattered. And after tomorrow, I'd finally be free to live the life I craved.

CHAPTER 2

STONE

*A*fter spending most of the night tossing and turning, sleep came in the early morning hours. Slumber's smothering embrace held me tight, dragging me into a dream that had replayed often since my arrival in Verona. A time long gone eclipsed the present, and I stepped into the life of another, no longer the hotel owner, but a busboy living with his father in the basement of this very building.

My arms laden with guests' luggage, I sidestepped a group of people checking into the hotel. My father was employed here, too, and happy with his lot in life. I was not. My dreams were bigger. This place, although extravagant, was not how I wanted to exist—fetching and carrying things for people with a better station than mine. One day, I vowed to make my fortune. I'd toyed with the idea of owning an inn. Perhaps not as grand as this one, but a successful business nonetheless.

"Mi scusi." I maneuvered around a group of gentlemen. That's when I saw her—a vision. Long, honey-blond hair artfully arranged with a few wavy tendrils around the face of

an angel. My heart skipped a beat then sped up, thundering in my ears.

An older couple stood beside her. They paled in comparison, despite their similar build and facial features. Slowing my stride, I caught snippets of their conversation, discovering her name was Francesca. I tore my attention from her for a brief second to scan for a suitor, a husband. There was no ring on her finger, no man by her side. But everyone noticed her.

She looked to be of similar age to me, perhaps a year or two younger than my nineteen years. As if in quicksand, I forced myself to move forward, the burden of the luggage nearly forgotten. *Look at me*, I implored her with my thoughts.

When her brilliant blue gaze collided with mine, she froze. Lush lips parted on a gasp, and an enchanting pink infused her high cheekbones. She had to have felt the connection too.

Her stunning features seared into my mind. I had to talk to her. If only I could. One look at those around her made it clear that it would not happen, at least, not at this moment. But I was inventive. I'd find the perfect opportunity to steal time with her.

Everything in my being pulled me toward her. *She's the one*. I was sure of it. Electricity charged the air. I recognized this moment for what it was—one where everything would change. Destiny.

The shrill beep of my alarm screeched, and I jackknifed in bed, ruthlessly ripped from sleep. I scrubbed my face with the palms of my hands before taking in the deep-red chairs, dresser, and double wood doors all visible from where I sat on the four-poster bed. I was in my room at the hotel, my latest project.

It was just another dream. She wasn't real. Even though my heart beat sluggishly from the loss of Francesca's presence—from the possibility of her.

Even with the physical grounding of my room—the hotel I owned rather than being employed in—I couldn't shake the haunting dreams, the vision of the girl, nor the chains of despair whenever I went anywhere near the basement. That, I avoided at all costs.

I forced myself to get up and get ready for a long day of work. Tiffany, my executive assistant would be out on maternity leave after tomorrow. There was a lot she and I had to cover before that happened, as well as acclimate her replacement to the workload.

The double doors to my room clicked shut behind me, and I made my way down the hall to the penthouse suite that we'd turned into our temporary offices. Tiffany would be a few minutes late. With her pregnancy, she was often tired, and I'd reduced her hours to try to ease some of her stress. That gave me enough time to make a dent in my emails and down a cup of coffee. Buried in my work, the first hour flew by.

"Wow, you look awful. What is it with this project?"

"Thank you, Tiffany." I spared her a glance from answering emails. "You, on the other hand, are glowing."

She snorted, and her curly hair bounced. "Spare me. I have cankles and heartburn. And the baby uses my bladder as a trampoline, or a punching bag." A puff of air pushed past her lips. "It'll be weird not coming in to work every day."

"You'll be a fantastic mom." I grinned, both happy and a little sad that she was leaving, even if it was only temporary. She was a great assistant. "You know you can take all the time you need with the baby. If you want to stay home longer, I'll always have a job for you."

"I know." Her voice softened. "Aaron and I've talked about

it. I want to come back, but only part-time, and not right away."

"Whatever you need." I pulled open my top right desk drawer and withdrew an envelope. "This is for you, Aaron, and the new baby." I'd gotten them a cleaning service for the year, yard maintenance, and gift cards for a few of her favorite stores.

Her eyes teared up as she looked inside. "Stone, this is too much."

"It isn't." She was the first executive assistant I could rely on for more than office work. There wasn't anything that was too much for her and her family. She'd become a friend and helped to keep me sane while I dealt with the cacophony that was this place. She'd even run interference with Celia when I was low on sleep and short of temper. I'd hired Celia as a favor to her uncle, who was on my board and a good man. She, on the other hand, was a problem. I rubbed my forehead, trying to drive her from my thoughts.

"What's going on?" Tiffany's brows scrunched together in worry. "You look stressed. Is it the dreams? Or did you go over the designs for the basement?"

I ground my teeth. I could barely bring myself to go down there, let alone go over the proposed plans by the design team. I'd also be forced to deal with Celia, who was a little too enthusiastic about spending time with me in any capacity. Something my mother encouraged since her best friend was Celia's mom. They'd been attempting to play matchmaker with us since I was young. But I knew Celia's ambitions well and wanted nothing to do with the matrimony-gold-digging-noose she wanted to slip over my head. "I didn't sleep well. And I'm not dealing with Celia right now."

Tiffany pursed her lips. "You did what you told her uncle you would do. You gave her a shot."

"Never mind about her." I leaned back in my chair and

got comfortable. We had a morning ritual where we'd spend several minutes going over anything she forgot to tell me from the day before due to pregnancy brain. "Have a seat and catch me up with what's happening tomorrow."

"Ah, tomorrow." A cheshire grin curved her mouth. "What are you going to do without me here?"

I narrowed my eyes at her, and a sliver of worry shot through me. "You did hire someone to fill in while you're on maternity leave, right?" She said she had, but with how tired and forgetful she was, I was kicking myself for not following up on that with my usually self-sufficient assistant.

"That's what I wanted to talk to you about. Her name is Adeline Rossi, and she's a sorority sister." She held up her palms facing me in defense over hiring someone fresh from graduating college. "Hear me out. She's young, yes, but she's incredibly smart. She skipped a few grades, had a full academic ride to my alma mater, and graduated with top honors."

"She has a high IQ." I shrugged. "That doesn't mean she knows about working with a Fortune 500 company like mine."

Her grin stretched impossibly wider. "Interesting that you say that. Adeline has had internships with Fortune 500 companies and even one with Stone Enterprises."

"That sound promising but—"

"Wait, there's more. She has a double major and two minors. I promise you, she's brilliant. From her work experience, she'll be able to handle my job without a problem. And… she speaks Italian. One of her father's employees spoke it fluently, and she picked up the language when she was young helping out with paperwork and phones at her dad's shop. She also took a few years of Italian in college."

"All right. If you trust she can keep up with the work, then I'm convinced." But could she handle whatever cursed this hotel, my moods, and the tenacious Celia?

Adeline

DUSK SETTLED LIKE A FINE WINE, CASTING A WARM GLOW OFF the old-world renaissance buildings. I hurried down the sidewalk, my heavy luggage bumping along behind me on squeaky wheels. I'd managed to grab a couple of hours of sleep on the flight from Chicago to Verona, Italy. At the airport, I changed from comfortable flats, yoga pants, and my "coffee, a hug in a cup" T-shirt to a crème blouse, black pencil skirt, and ankle strap dress shoes—not the easiest to walk in, especially since my ankles buckled a few times. My heels clicked on the sidewalk, mingling with the other pedestrian traffic. I had the cab drop me off a few blocks from the hotel so I could walk a little through the town and soak up the atmosphere of the surrounding area.

Excitement held some of the exhaustion at bay, and I wished Eileen were here with me. For my first time away from my hometown, this was incredible. Italy was a symphony of rich espresso beans, the aroma of baked bread, infectious laughter, music, and the joyful chaos that saturated the city. My spirit soared. This job would unlock so many doors, allowing for travel and new experiences that I longed for.

Up ahead, the Hotel Destino rose in dark and delightful majesty. Arches and Juliet balconies spoke of history. Romance emanated from the artful arrangement of brick and stone that dated back centuries. The building was in beautiful shape. My steps quickened in anticipation of stepping inside and being enveloped in what must house breathtaking frescoes, elaborate décor, and five floors of glorious opportunity.

If I proved myself in this temporary job, I could very well be on the path to managing a Stone Enterprises hotel. The thought of being responsible for the day-to-day operations of one of Stone Crenshaw's hotels made me giddy with anticipation.

The front entryway was in sight, and as I skirted around a man in a black suit, I narrowly missed his briefcase, pummeling me in the knee. Instead, I teetered on my heels, and by some miracle, regained my balance. With a hard yank, I forced my rolling suitcase to return behind me, instead of careening wildly on one wheel as it had been. I didn't let the stranger's carelessness stop me from my destination, or to quell my excitement. My pace slowed as I took in the hotel up close. *I'm here.* I couldn't believe it. With a deep inhale, I stepped forward, ready to embrace my carefully planned destiny.

The gentle trickle of water drew my attention, and I turned my head in the direction of the source. A simple fountain gurgled, and my breath caught as a sense of familiarity stirred from the timeless entryway of the hotel. With my free hand, I reached for a necklace that I knew I'd toyed with thousands of times. It wasn't there.

Then a flash of light blinded me, and I stopped in my tracks, blinking repeatedly. Déjà vu hit me hard, and I swore I heard the swelling strains of violins and cellos in a haunting melody. Black spots crowded my sight, and I swayed. A memory tugged, and I wanted to follow it, allowing the darkness to invade my mind further.

Lightheaded, my eyelids fluttered and I stumbled forward. A deep voice snapped in bone-chilling familiarity near my ear. Like an invisible thread, he anchored me here.

There was something about the encounter I didn't immediately recognize but that resonated in my soul.

I fought the pull to unconsciousness while my mind straddled between the vision desperate to be seen and the man's insistent voice in a fuzzy void that spun out of focus. Knees buckling, I went down, helpless against the dizziness and a sense of longing I couldn't place.

The world shifted, and I slammed into something hard. A wall? A deep, gravelly tone penetrated the haze, and I blinked to clear it away. Not a wall, but a man. Gunmetal eyes met my own, and the world snapped back around me in brutal clarity. *Holy mother of…* Heat crept up my neck. I surely resembled a lobster while wrapped in a smoking-hot stranger's embrace. I put my hands on his substantial chest and eased back as a bolt of electricity shot through me at his touch, raising the fine hairs all over my body. *What was that?*

"Are you okay?"

His sinful baritone yanked me from my stupor, and I untangled myself from his arms. I missed the connection instantly. "Yes, of course." Just mortified. "Thanks for breaking my fall. Jet lag…" I cast another glance at the fountain, unable to shake the weird thing that'd happened.

"Do we know each other?" From head to toe, his gaze traveled over me.

"No. No, I've never been to Italy before." Realizing I'd let go of my heavy suitcase, I bent and grabbed the handle from the sidewalk, peeking at the hotel behind him. The foot traffic had thinned. At least there were fewer people to witness the awkwardness of my arrival. And hopefully, no one saw whom I would be working with.

"We must have met—"

"No. I've never been to Italy. I'm sure we haven't."

His deep sex-and-sin voice made me want to stay in his

arms, as if that was exactly where I belonged. *Ah, stop!* That wasn't me. Eileen and my sorority sisters, yes, but not me. I was focused, if not jet-lagged. That had to be the reason he was affecting me so much.

I sidestepped him, yet his hand remained on my arm, a conduit that linked us on a cellular level that I wasn't sure I understood. "Thanks again." I gave a little smile as his penetrating stare sent a wave of shivers over me. *My sorority sisters would find him devastating.* But I wouldn't let the odd sense of attraction interfere with why I was here. I had bigger things to embrace inside, and I couldn't wait to get in there. While I appreciated him saving me from certain road rash on my face, there was zero time for me to stand around chatting. That wasn't why I was here.

I took in the hotel, fighting the pull of the powerful man that stood too near. This was the path I'd chosen to succeed —a career, not a romantic encounter or a boyfriend. With my degree under my belt and the employment opportunity, I planned to rise out of poverty and create a name for myself in the business world. I would leave my mark.

I drew my arm back, off-balance from the strange electric awareness his touch caused, my face still on fire, and he frowned. "I'm fine." I held up my hands and swayed. His hand shot back out to grip my elbow.

"You're not fine," he growled, impatience lining his tightly pressed lips.

My spine snapped straight, and I hitched my new bag higher on my shoulder. "I am."

Silence stretched between us, and I fought the urge to offer more of an explanation. He was very intimidating with his six foot two or three inches of height and commanding presence. I needed to end this stare-off. "Thanks again," I said, then pivoted to the right and hurried to the front entrance to the hotel. Wonder hit me as I crossed over the threshold and into the elegant foyer. This was where my dreams would be realized.

CHAPTER 3

ADELINE

hrough the windowpane, stars sprinkled the sky in a midnight blanket, and my eyelids grew heavy as I lay in the plush bed in the most gorgeous room I'd ever slept in. It'd taken two hours for me to relax enough even to come close to sleep. Each time my eyes drifted shut, colors swirled, intermingled with a man's voice, and I'd jolted awake. This time, I eased into slumber, the deep cadence of his whisper lulling me into my dream—*to him.*

My new corset pinched, and I must have made another sound of distress. *Madre* cast a disapproving glance my way. Our skirts swooshed in a heavy fall of silk—pale blue for me and champagne for hers—as we left our rooms for the parlor on the first floor of the inn. The new dresses were the latest fashion, a gift from *Padre,* and I was to wear it to my chaperoned meeting with Angelo. My parents were hoping for a match as his family was cultured and rivaled ours in social status, finance, and power.

I didn't care about any of that. The heady scent of flowers filled the air as we meandered under high arches, and beneath a ceiling mural of the sky, I stretched my fingers on the opposite side of *Madre* to run over to the grand piano, itching to take a seat and test the ivory. As we passed the lovely fresco landscape in the opulent foyer, I longed to gaze upon the art. People mingled, and the soft tinkle of laughter buoyed my flagging spirits.

I wasn't ready to meet Angelo, in particular, because of the rumors of his boorish manner and wandering eye. *Madre* overlooked such things, saying the social status would outweigh any indiscretions and that she and *Padre* wanted me settled. I disagreed but only in my head. My older sister was already married with her second baby on the way. *Madre* wanted me to follow suit. My mind circled back to the bellhop.

Tall, dark, and handsome drew my focus from the corner of the room. Travel trunks in tow, his strong arms bulged, and my mouth went dry. As he neared, my heart rate sped up. When we'd first arrived at the inn, he'd taken our luggage to our rooms. Even then, I couldn't keep from following his movements, peeking at his face and warm brown eyes. When my parents weren't looking, he'd flashed me a smile that'd made me breathless. This was the man I wanted an introduction to. But it wasn't meant to be. Even I knew that a bellhop was too far below our rung on the social ladder.

From the corner of my eye, I tracked him as he approached. Mouth dry, I nearly stumbled as we stepped from the narrow hardwood floors to the handwoven European rug. His path hadn't changed; would he speak to us? Would *Madre* allow it?

"Pardon me, ladies, my name is Cristiano, and my *padrone* bid me to suggest you visit Casa di Giulietta, our famed home of Shakespeare's Juliet before you attend the opera this evening."

Madre answered that we would indeed do so while I devoured Cristiano's stunning features. His boss? I didn't think he spoke the truth that the suggestion to visit was from his *padrone*. Not by the subtle hints of inflection he wove into his speech to *Madre*—but they weren't meant for her. They were meant for me.

When *Madre* wasn't watching, he sent me a secret grin and opened his palm to reveal a simple necklace with a pendant of Saint Valentine dangling from the delicate silver chain. I wanted to sigh from the heat spreading throughout my body. He made me feel flushed, excited, and rebellious. My sisters may be content in their marriages, but I was not inclined to be swayed by who my parents deemed socially acceptable over love.

My cell phone's shrill alarm blared, ruthlessly yanking me from the most intricate dream I'd had in months, years maybe. This place, with its nineteenth-century décor, was to blame. It had to be. In record time, I managed to drag myself from the heavenly bed, shake off the odd night, and get dressed for my first day on the job.

Soft light spilled from sconces strategically placed along the hall, and I had to work to see the bulbs in place rather than the way they'd flickered with candlelight in my dream. I smoothed my hand down my deep-gray pencil skirt, one of three that I owned, then knocked on the door to Stone Crenshaw's office suite. He had one of two of the penthouse suites on the top floor, where Tiffany had told me to go. The sound of my knuckles rapping against the door sent another rush of nervous excitement through me.

As I waited, the anticipation to meet him built. Very few pictures had been taken of him. From what I'd read, he didn't care for the publicity. And while he was on the cover of Forbes for his company's rise to fame, and also on Page Six as the most eligible bachelor, his features had often been caught in shadow, further enhancing his air of unattainability, of mystery.

The door whipped open, and I couldn't help but mirror the grin on Tiffany's face as she stepped aside so I could enter. Careful not to nudge her baby bump, I shimmied through the entrance then waited for her to tell me where to go.

"I'm so thrilled you're here." Her smile stretched impossibly wider. "I'll walk you through everything today, then after, you can reach me by phone if you have questions."

"Okay." I twisted my hands together in front of me to still the urge to tug at my pale-blue sweater.

She squeezed my shoulder. "You'll be fine. Once you get the hang of things, working with Stone will be a piece of cake." With an eye roll, she groaned. "Now I want chocolate cake. This baby is going to make me so fat."

"You're adorable and not in any way overweight." She really was. Her skin had this amazing glow, her eyes sparkled, and her cheerful mood was infectious. Ever since we'd talked on the phone, I'd connected with her, which was probably another reason I'd landed this job. It was probable that the position was temporary, but a stepping stone nonetheless. "From the back, I couldn't even tell you were pregnant." From what she'd told me last conversation, this was her first pregnancy, and she and her husband were thrilled for the baby's arrival, which was due in about a month.

"Well, I'm sort of done. My feet are killing me, and I have to pee every twenty minutes. Don't even get me started on what happens if I sneeze or cough." She rolled her eyes. "I'm ready for this baby to be born."

"Not much longer." I took a moment to glance around as she led me into a large living room that had a mahogany desk near the entrance to the balcony. Tall windows showcased a glimpse of the Adige River and the Roman influence in the history of the surrounding homes and buildings. "Wow, that's the view we get to see every day?"

"It is. And it sets the mood. My husband and I were not immune. Romance permeates the air."

I laughed as she smoothed her hand over her stomach. From my walk through the town before arriving last night, I understood what she meant. Verona was where soul mates found one another. There were so many people out for a stroll, and I'd felt a natural high.

Snapping back to why I was here, I followed her to the desk that had a computer, two iPads, her cell phone, and a bunch of documents stacked to the side. "Grab that chair over there and pull it next to mine."

After I settled into the seat next to Tiffany, she went over everything I was to do. And there was a lot. An hour had gone by, and I was still taking notes, in between her answering the phone and setting up a few meetings for Stone. I could hear his deep baritone in the next room, but I had yet to lay eyes on him, which was probably a good thing. I was nervous enough as is.

Tiffany nudged me. "Can you run another mug of coffee to Stone? He usually takes one about now, and the less I have to be on my feet…"

"Oh, of course. I shouldn't wait until he's off the phone?"

She shook her head, sending her dark curls to fall over her shoulders. "He's a bear without it." With a wave of her hand toward the kitchen, I got to my feet. "He takes it black. Just lightly knock then enter."

The kitchen was elegant with white granite and gray specks through the design that contrasted well with the dark cabinets. With Stone's mug in hand, I did as Tiffany asked, despite my nerves.

My fingers squeezed the handle of his cup tightly as I opened the door then made my way to his desk. It was another big room, furnished as an office. The rich, *familiar* tones of his voice lured me to him, and I extended my arm to set the coffee next to him. He shifted, and his forearm brushed my hand as he turned to type something on his laptop. His features came into view, and I froze. *It's him.*

My gut twisted as I realized Stone Crenshaw was the handsome man who'd saved me from face planting last night. *How did I not recognize him?* A tremor ran through my body, and my hand shook, sloshing a few drops of coffee onto a document on his desk.

Obsidian eyes snapped to mine and flared in recognition. I sucked in a breath. He ripped the cup from my grasp before I spilled anymore on his papers. Then he stood and gave me his back. He continued to bark orders into his Bluetooth as he walked to the windows.

Spotting a box of Kleenex on a small table next to the couch, I dabbed at the offending splash of liquid. Effectively dismissed, I tucked tail and hurried out of the office, closing the door with a soft click behind me.

Tiffany finished up a call and got to her feet with a groan, hands on her lower back, her eyelids fluttered closed. "I want to show you around, and I could use a stretch." She handed me an iPad, and I followed her out the door, my face on fire from the encounter with Stone.

When she turned to me, worry lines creased her normally smooth forehead. "Oh no, what happened?"

"Nothing other than I have yet to make a good impression on the boss. It seems he's the one who caught me when I, um, lost my balance in front of the hotel last night. And today, I spilled a few drops of coffee on his desk."

Tiffany burst out laughing. "Oh, you definitely made an impression."

I gave her the side-eye. "Thanks, that's very helpful."

"It'll be fine. I promise." Soft chuckles continued as we got into the elevator to head to the second floor. "He hasn't told me to fire you, so I wouldn't worry." A ding sounded as we stopped moving, then the doors opened onto a construction site.

"How far along is the renovation?"

"The top three floors are mostly done, but no furniture has been brought in. The goal is to keep the décor close to its original design." Tiffany's mouth pinched. "We've had some issues with vendors… and the lead designer."

"I take it this is where I'll get involved?" The set to her pinched lips and strained features told me more than what she'd said. This would be a problem, a big one. My heels clicked as we walked toward a tall brunette in a ridiculous formfitting dress and Manolo Blahnik heels. Just looking at her sophisticated hairstyle and obvious designer outfit made me want to turn and walk away.

My clothes were discount, not designer, and my hair was in a smoothed-back ponytail rather than a sleek cut like hers that stopped in a silky fall, barely brushing her shoulders. I should've attempted that chignon Eileen did for me on one occasion. But I'd woken late, and this was the best I could do.

My nonexistent budget and worn clothes were fine at college. Not so much in the working world. I'd had to shop at discount stores and even garage sales to scrape together a semi-passible wardrobe. I was counting on buying a few nicer pieces after my first paycheck. But designer? Nope. It wasn't worth it, not when I needed to save money and pay off my horrendous school loans. The full academic scholarship I'd received hadn't covered everything: not books, food, or the massive medical bills I was saddled with after Dad died.

A chime rang, and Tiffany swiped a finger across her iPad, bringing the screen to life. A few more taps, and she pulled up an email. "Oh, why did IT send this to me?" She scrunched her nose and messed with the screen another second, then a ping sounded on mine. "They sent me your username and password. I forwarded it to you."

Tiffany led me forward, and we closed the distance between the statuesque woman and us. "Celia. This is Adeline, Mr. Crenshaw's executive assistant covering for me while I'm on maternity leave."

I held out my hand, juggling the electronic device at the same time. It slipped as Celia reached out. Instead of grasping my hand, her fingers curled around my iPad, and she rudely read the email Tiffany had sent with my login information. "Adeline?" Her gaze traveled from my head to my shoes. "Hmm, you look like a Brittney to me. Maybe Addy is better fitting." She transferred the electronic device to her other hand, shook mine then gave it back.

My smile froze. That nickname Addy didn't bring good memories. "Well, I'm not, just Adeline." I cradled the mini computer to my chest, the email still open—what a bitch. There was no mistaking the Barbie category she was pigeon-holing me for.

Tiffany's spine straightened, pushing out her small round belly. "Careful, Celia. *Adeline* will be the go-between for all approvals."

"Why would I go through her? She's new, doesn't have Stone's vision." She snapped. "I'll correspond with Stone instead."

"*Mr. Crenshaw* turned all renovation approvals over to me, and now to Adeline." Tiffany's voice hardened. "You will not bother him unless you'd like to look for another job."

Arms crossed, Celia's cold gaze jerked to my face again, and a chill crawled down my spine. With very few words, I'd made an enemy with this one. Although it was doubtful she could compromise my position with the company. I mean, what could she possibly do?

CHAPTER 4

ADELINE

Tiffany and I sat in the outdoor section of the restaurant overlooking the Adige River on my second day of work. After the craziness of yesterday, she'd decided to come in for half the day to make sure I was acclimating. The sound of people chatting and the hauntingly romantic strains of a street musician's violin a block over added to the experience. Already, I loved Verona—my job, not so much. But I'd change that and make it mine. I had a plan after all.

My phone pinged with a text, and when I saw it was Tommy, I blocked it. This job was too important to me, and I didn't want to deal with a repeat conversation of the same thing. Besides, he didn't love me in the way he thought he did. The real problem was the superstitions he imagined. I didn't need to be at his games to ensure his success. He did that all on his own.

I toyed with my necklace Mom bought me when I was young, the weight of the pendant comforting between my fingers. Pushing the past aside, I let go of the jewelry and took another sip of my drink to wash down the last of my meal.

Our lunch finished, Tiffany stood and wrapped her arms around me. "You've got this."

I returned her squeeze, careful of her baby bump. My head spun from the proverbial baton she'd passed. This was it. I would run the show from here on out.

"Oh! I almost forgot." She rolled her eyes. "I have pregnancy brain so bad. About an hour ago, I got a call that the meeting for Stone at the Bianca Hotel was moved up to today. I changed it on the calendar but spaced giving him a verbal heads-up. Please make sure to do that."

"I will, as soon as I get back."

Her shoulders dropped an inch, and the strain around her mouth eased as she told me about the change in schedule. "Great. He's insane about this purchase. That's the only thing to be careful about. Anything regarding the Bianca is a priority. He hasn't been sleeping well and has been increasingly grouchy the longer we're onsite in Verona."

"Good to know."

She tapped her chin with a French manicured fingernail. "I'm trying to think about anything else you should know. Stone is onsite, sleeping in the other penthouse suite. In addition to the office one and yours, none of the other rooms are furnished yet. You'll have the unpleasant task of approving Celia's orders soon."

"I'll handle it." I smiled, trying to ease her worry.

"Watch out for her. She has a thing for Stone and can make a nuisance of herself."

Wonderful. "No worries, I'll manage her."

"You'll do great." She squeezed my hands. "I'm heading home. Call if you have questions, okay? I live here on the outskirts of town with my husband so don't feel like I'm too far away and can't help out."

I assured her I would call if I had questions, then we

parted, each going in opposite directions. I took my time walking back to the hotel where Mr. Crenshaw would be in the middle of a conference call, according to the calendar we shared.

The melody of the violin faded the farther I went, but the magic of the city remained. For the first time since Mom died, I felt at peace.

Hotel Destino loomed before me, and I slowed down to take in the beauty of it for a few unhurried minutes. Once inside, I went to the elevators not being used by the construction guys. It didn't take long until the doors slid open with a soft chime, and I stepped out and into the huge suite where Stone had his office set up, and now mine.

With the tablet in hand, I cautiously approached his door where I could hear him barking orders to the unlucky recipient on the other end of the conference call. A light tap and I pushed the door open, pausing at the threshold.

Instead of finding him seated behind the mahogany desk, or pacing like he was prone to do, he sat in one of the chairs that looked like they'd be great for reading and sipping a glass of wine. If I could, I would take that comfy seat back to my room to do exactly that.

Three large windows that showcased the amazing view did little to drag my attention from his sinful good looks. His thick hair made my fingers twitch with want of running through it. Then there was his graphite eyes and olive skin that were in contrast to my light tones. I rapped my knuckles slightly on the frame. With a brief nod, he acknowledged me and motioned for me to enter. I gave myself a mental shake to clear the thoughts that I should not have about my boss.

Head down, I tapped on the link to the shared calendar while moving closer to him. My heels clicked on the hardwood floors. Everything was going fine until I stepped on something that rolled out from under the ball of my foot. Pain shot up to my ankle. Stumbling, I wobbled and took another stuttering-step before losing my balance. I pitched forward, my phone flew from my grasp—and I face-planted in his crotch.

"*Oomph.*"

Ohshitohshitohshit! Hands on his thighs, I pushed back and removed my face from his lap. I gained a couple of inches in retreat until a painful tug on my hair stopped me from shifting another inch. Scorching heat climbed my neck. My horrified gaze flicked to his. A muscle pulsed along his jaw, and his free hand was at the side of my head, caught.

"I'll have to call you back," he bit out between clenched teeth to the person on the phone. "Hold still. My watch is stuck."

My pulse hammered at breakneck speed as he worked to disengage himself. Trapped, I stared helplessly at him.

"What the hell happened?"

"I-I stepped on something. Tripped." I felt like a caged bird. Why was I so nervous around him? Slowly, I lifted my hands and untwisted my hair from the semi-secure bun. There was no way he was getting his watch out with it up like this. With a few twists, I got the band out, and my hair tumbled down my back. I brushed his hands away to work on separating the strands entwined in the silver links of his watchband.

My fingers worked furiously to free myself from this position. Would he fire me? I mean, my face was literally… I risked another glance at him. The angry tick was gone. Instead, his dark eyes burned with something else, shifting restlessly over my face, then hair, then back. This was bad. I had to smooth things over, get back to a professional existence where he barely acknowledged me. Something like this would not further my career.

It would end it.

I freed the last few strands, picked up the thankfully undamaged tablet, and stood on shaky legs. "The calendar is updated, but I came in here to tell you that the Bianca bid meeting was changed from tomorrow to this evening."

"Fuck." His face was a mask of fury as he stretched to his full height. "Find out if they have another buyer and who it is."

"Of course." I turned too fast and swayed. His hand curled around my elbow to steady me, and jolts of electricity shot along my arm. Mumbling thanks, I pulled free then hurried out of his office. Once past the doorway, I sucked in much needed air. His touch may have fallen away, but not the lasting effects. My hands shook as I looked up the phone number for the executive assistant Tiffany dealt with regarding the acquisition of the Venice property. Two rings, and Rose answered.

"Mr. Mariucci's office."

"Hi Rose, this is Adeline, calling on behalf of Stone Crenshaw."

"Oh, yes, you're Tiffany's temporary replacement. I spoke to her earlier this morning about the change in schedule for the meeting."

"That's what I was calling about. Mr. Crenshaw would like to inquire if there are any other interested parties."

"There is another gentleman and his wife, whose bid Mr. Mariucci is entertaining."

"Would you mind sharing who they are?" I had already checked that the stipulation of the bidding process allowed for full disclosure of all interested parties.

"Of course. The other offer will be made by George and Anne Fielding."

"Thank you, Rose. If there are any new developments, would you please email or call me with them?" I made sure she had my contact information.

We said our goodbyes, and I buzzed Stone's intercom, relaying the details as soon as he answered. It was that or go back to his office to tell him to his face, which I didn't want to do on the heels of what happened a few minutes ago. My face still burned from embarrassment, and my stomach was tied in knots.

"And his wife?" Stone's deep voice crackled with anger, and my back snapped straight.

"Yes, that's what I was told."

Silence stretched between us for a few seconds, where I wondered if I should disconnect or wait for his direction first. It didn't take long. He hung up and then appeared at the opening to his office. The room shrunk with his commanding presence. He leaned against the doorframe, and his calculating look sent shivers up my spine.

"Pack a bag." His features gave away nothing, except for a speculative gleam in his eyes. "You'll be going with me."

I nodded, replacing the receiver I clung to back in its cradle. "I'll purchase an additional ticket." We didn't have too long before we needed to leave if we wanted to be at the meeting on time. The train would take approximately an hour and a half.

"One other thing, Adeline." I froze like a rabbit caught in a predator's sight. "I'll have some paperwork my lawyer will have drafted for you to sign before we arrive in Venice. This new information about my competition calls for a different game plan. You'll be accompanying me as my fiancée."

What? "Excuse me?" My head knocked back from the verbal blow he'd delivered.

"I won't lose out on this purchase." His voice lowered, softened, and was scarier than when he was snapping orders to the unfortunate people on his conference calls. "Mariucci is blinded by family values. I won't allow the scale to tip in my adversary's favor because he's married."

"I hardly think that his marital status would affect Mr. Mariucci's decision, nor do I want to be pretend engaged to you." I cringed at how that sounded. But really, I had no desire to go down that path—again.

Stone pushed off the door jam, closing the distance between us. I tensed, suddenly grateful for the desk that maintained some level of separation.

"His wife will be present in the meeting, will she not?"

Dammit. "Yes." Tiffany wasn't kidding about his fanatical behavior surrounding the Venice deal. But engaged?

"Then the rules of the game have changed. This is not negotiable, Adeline. It is merely a business relationship. I'll get what I want out of it… the building. And you'll enjoy the perks of my credit card." He paused, most likely taking in my pinched lips and furious stare.

"No." I had enough of the men in my life thinking they could manipulate me. But I could use this situation and make it work in my favor. "If I go along with this, I want something else in return."

His brow furrowed, and he remained perfectly still.

Sensing his curiosity, I pushed my luck. "This will be a confidential arrangement between us. No one will ever hear a word of it. And *if* I do sign the contract, I want a stipulation added that I'll be in charge of this hotel, or one of my choosing when our deal is over."

A wolfish smile curved his lips, and I found myself holding my breath. I was in over my head. Going toe-to-toe with a man like Stone was a huge risk.

"Should you hold up your end of the deal, I'll put an amendment in for a leadership position, if you have the necessary skills. The pretend part will be confidential, our engagement will not. That's all I'm willing to offer."

Hmm, I bet this would help him with Celia's obsession. "Fine. I'd like time to look over the contract before I agree."

Business arrangement or not, I had a feeling this proposition would end badly for one of us—namely me.

CHAPTER 5

ADELINE

The hum of the water taxi filled the silence between Stone and me as we were ushered to our destination along the Venice shore. My gaze darted over the coast, taking in the wide expanse of beach flanking the majestic hotel that Stone had dreams of owning. A gust of warm air swept over the water, making Stone's suit jacket flap and teasing a few tendrils of my hair.

Nausea churned in my gut, threatening to take me to my knees if I thought too long about what the hell had happened. Stone and I—because I was not going to call him Mr. Crenshaw while fake engaged—had taken a train and then a water taxi to the lagoon that met the shoreline in front of the luxurious Bianca hotel. Venice was the city of canals. The Bianca was built on Venice-Lido, which housed the best beach in front of the hotel, and fed into a lagoon and the Adriatic Sea. It was a spectacular location with Adriatic-facing beaches. A ten-minute water taxi was needed to travel between the hotel and the many Venice attractions.

My overactive mind continued to whirl. How was I going

to do this, be so close to him, when he made me feel so utterly unlike myself?

The three-carat platinum antique diamond ring circled my finger like a shackle rather than a priceless heirloom meant to signify a lifelong promise.

I avoided his direction while I wrestled with the ramifications of the contract I'd read over—and signed—on the train. I'd had the option to back out. But when this fake engagement dissolved after Stone achieved his goals, I would have my pick between three of his hotels to manage, essentially fast-tracking my career. Although, he'd added the stipulation of intense training by his top manager Leif in their Swiss hotel location before I assumed my new role. That didn't concern me. So far, everything workwise had been a breeze. What concerned me was being in close proximity to Stone.

My mind continued to yo-yo while I wrestled with the decision I made. My goals were within my grasp. Then why did resentment burn in my gut? This would be an even faster way to achieve my objective, to establish myself and secure my future, and never have to rely on anyone or forfeit my dreams. Even so, I couldn't shake the sense of impending doom.

The water taxi docked with the wind on our backs, teasing loose a few tendrils of silvery blond hair to twist free of my chignon and dance in front of my face. Stone extended his hand to help me off the gently rocking vessel, and I shivered at his touch. Stone cleared his throat, and I fought the urge to shift my focus, to lose myself in his stormy gray eyes. I wasn't ready. Not yet.

With a gentle touch, he brushed the few strands behind my ear, and I suppressed the shiver that wasn't due to the light breeze. Then he spoke, his voice soothing like a full-body caress, and electricity shot along every inch of me. What was it that pulled me toward him?

"This deal is crucial." His statement rang with determination. "I'm going to need you to read the room and go with my cues in front of the other people present."

"I understand." He'd already stressed this in the contract and verbally on the train. I had to fight from rolling my eyes against the waves of energy coming off him. I could appreciate his drive. So long as we kept our interactions to strictly business, then I could do this. And really, I should take full advantage of my situation, and I met his gaze with an evil grin, batting my eyelashes, hoping to infuse some levity to our situation. "As your fiancée, would I carry my bags in?"

He grunted his response but tossed the strap of my overnight bag on his shoulder. "From my research—"

"You mean Tiffany's?" I widened my eyes, feigning innocence. Yep, I was going to have fun with this. No more stressing.

The same muscle from earlier jumped along his jawline. "No. Like I was saying…" He shot me a glare. "Mariucci is a family man. With Fielding's bid, that will come into play. I'll introduce you as my executive assistant. The story we'll tell is that we met when you interned for my company. After you finished with that and graduated college, we started dating."

"That won't work for me." It was another case of needing a man to get ahead, and while I was okay to use his fake engagement contract as a springboard in my career, I was not willing to compromise my reputation. "I won't have it known I didn't get the job on my merit. And aren't you a little old for me?" He wasn't, but I wanted to know his age. "Not to mention, I graduated days before I took this position."

The corner of his mouth twitched, and I narrowed my eyes at him.

"Very well. And I'm twenty-nine—not too old."

It was that easy? Hmm, I should have gotten more from

him out of going along with his charade. He was right, though, seven years of an age difference wasn't bad. I gritted my teeth and lengthened my stride to keep up with his longer one. When we were almost to the doors of the hotel, I tugged on his sleeve. "I need to swap shoes." Now that we were here, I wanted to change out of the flats I'd worn for practicality and into the heels I had in my bag. I kept hold of his arm while I switched shoes, scowling at his amused expression.

He held the door open for me, and I breezed past him. Or I'd like to say I did. My heel caught on the threshold and, of course, I tripped. His arm wrapped around my waist. Air whooshed from my lungs, and he pulled my back against his wall of a chest. He bent down so his mouth brushed against my ear, and I shivered—again.

"If you're going to wear heels you can't walk in unaided, then I'll need to hold onto you." His voice infused with repressed laughter. "We wouldn't want to have a repeat of what happened earlier in my office today."

No, that we would not. My brain shorted out while he shifted so his free arm wrapped around my waist, the bags over his opposite shoulder. The close proximity to so much *male* kept me mute the entire way up to the conference room where the meeting was scheduled. Stone detached himself from me and set our luggage in the entryway as Rose, Mr. Mariucci's executive assistant, greeted and ushered us in.

Another couple was at the table. The man, I presumed was George Fielding, was partially balding and had snapped his cold, calculating gaze to mine. His wife, Anne, sat beside him with perfect, honey-gold hair arranged in a twist. Her updo highlighted her flawless makeup. Diamonds dripped from her ears, neck, and adorned several of her fingers. I wasn't spared a second from her uninterested perusal—until she caught sight of Stone.

I was intrigued until she practically drooled at the sight of him. My mind snapped back to hyper-alert at her coy smile. Annoyance crackled beneath my skin. Our engagement may be fake, but there was no way I'd let her think she had any power over the man who supposedly wanted to spend the rest of his life with me. Yep, I got the irony. I didn't care.

I let my hand smooth the sleeve of his suit coat, consciously flashing the rock on my finger as I did so. Mr. Mariucci walked in as Stone turned to me with an amused grin. With his hand on my elbow, he pulled out my chair, most likely so I wouldn't face-plant trying to get into the seat myself.

Already, I could tell our competition lacked genuine warmth, so I focused on softening my features as I leaned back in my chair, my shoulder brushing against Stone's. His fingers curled around the back of my neck, stilling my movements. I fought against the heated reaction every time he touched me.

"Good evening, gentlemen and ladies." Mr. Mariucci extended his hand first to George then his wife. When Mr. Mariucci shifted his focus to Stone, I flattened my left hand on the table to push to my feet.

"Please, don't get up." Mr. Mariucci grinned down at me. After shaking Stone's hand, he reached across and grasped mine. "I don't believe we've had the pleasure of meeting."

Rose entered and got Anne settled with the Pellegrino she'd requested, taking her focus off of the three of us for a few moments.

"We have not." I returned his mischievous grin. "I've spoken to Rose a time or two since Tiffany, Stone's executive assistant, went on maternity leave." I threaded my fingers together and set them on the table, leaning forward as we spoke. There was no way he could miss the diamond winking at him.

"Have you worked for Stone long?"

Stone took his seat next to me as Mariucci did as well across from the four of us. "Her position was in a different department, which is how we first met."

Mariucci's focus fell to my hand, and I took that cue to give Stone's a quick squeeze. "We didn't plan to work in the same office, but he needed me to fill in for Tiffany, temporarily." I played my part, at least well enough, so they were convinced. "And to be honest, it's been nice spending extra time together."

"You two are engaged?" George deadpanned.

I met his and his wife's suspicious expressions with a light laugh. "We are! And after coming to this beautiful floating city, I'm hoping to talk Stone into taking me sightseeing." Take that Fieldings. Stone wasn't the only one who'd done his homework about the hotel owners and their love of Venice.

Anne pursed her lips then turned to Stone. "Didn't I see you with someone else at the cancer fundraiser a few months back?"

I put my hand on Stone's arm, pressing down so he knew I'd take this hit. "Oh, you mean Satan's Mistress? Excuse me. I don't know why I can't—" I waved my hand around as if trying to draw her name from the air. "So sorry, can't seem to get her name out."

"Sylvia," George delivered, his expression not at all amused while his wife's mouth hung open.

"Yes." I snapped my fingers. "That's the one! Wasn't she solely after your money, darling?" I turned to Stone.

"Hmm."

"I'm sorry I pushed you to take her instead of me to that function."

"I should have gone alone."

"Well." I winked at him. "Everything worked out in the end."

"What does that make you?" Anne found her voice again. "Somehow not after his billions?"

"No." I let all amusement fade to hammer home the next mic drop. "I insisted on a prenup. After the gold diggers that came before me, I never wanted him to have any doubt I was marrying him for love, not his money."

Mr. Mariucci chuckled. "You, dear, must meet my wife, Margaret. I know you two will get along famously."

"I'd be delighted to." I notched my head at Stone. "Maybe she can help me convince my workaholic fiancé that we need to stay a few days in Venice." *And that's how you do it!* I entwined my fingers with Stone's in preparation for my closing line. "I'd love for our wedding to be here."

CHAPTER 6

ADELINE

*C*aramel latte in hand, I took a fortifying sip before setting it on my desk and walking over to deliver Stone's black coffee. There would be no tripping incidents today. I wore my low wedge-heeled boots with yoga-type work pants. They looked exactly like dress slacks but were way more comfortable. Paired with a plum, silk blouse and my dark-framed faux glasses, I thought I looked sophisticated.

I carefully placed his coffee on his desk while he issued orders on this morning's conference call. That would be the hotel manager in California. I had a mile-long list of things to do today, including moving a few scheduled meetings from Saturday to Monday or Tuesday for Stone, considering we would be going back to Venice for the weekend. Our calendars had not aligned with Vince and Margaret Mariucci for dinner, and I hadn't been able to convince him to stay in Venice longer than a single night. We left at first light. Regardless, I planned to take full advantage of our current situation and drag him sightseeing with me when we returned.

Between sips of coffee heaven, I went through the list of changes Stone wanted to his agenda. Made phone calls, rescheduled, and organized his day, then ran a profit and loss statement he had been waiting on for too long from the San Francisco branch. Spotting several problem areas, I made notes on my report on suggested alternative solutions to implement.

That brought me to the next item on my day, the one I was dreading—checking in with Celia. She had yet to respond to my inquiries about the purchase orders submitted. For whatever reason—my guess was Stone's obsession with the Venice hotel—he didn't want to deal with anything regarding the renovation past the initial approval, which was long since completed. I'd already reviewed his notes about the décor and atmosphere he expected the design team to achieve. It was simple, elegant, and old-world.

With that, why were purchases for modern door handles out there? Celia was going to be a problem. Pushing up from my desk, I grabbed my company iPad and headed down to find her.

They were on the second floor, and when I stepped off the elevator, Celia was leaning against a table full of boxes and flipping through a magazine. *Was that Page Six?*

"Celia." My voice cracked like a whip and startled more than my intended target. "These are the wrong door handles." I firmly placed a copy of the purchase order on the table next to where her hip rested. "Please return them and order the correct ones."

"I think not." Disdain dripped from her cultured, nasty voice, and her gaze traveled from my head to toes. "If Stone—"

"Mr. Crenshaw." I locked down on my feelings of inadequacy over my clothes that were not designer brands like hers. How much I spent didn't matter, what did was that I could outthink her any day.

"—wanted something different, he can speak with me." She waved her hand toward the elevator in dismissal.

So, she wanted a power play? I hardened my expression, aware that the three other women on her team were hovering nearby. "It's simple, Celia, make the change, or your purchase privileges will be revoked. You have one hour to get this accomplished. I expect an update at that time."

I pivoted on my heels and stepped into the elevator as one of the construction crew was exiting. Perfect timing. As the doors closed, I held her enraged stare. The ride up was spent pulling up the other women on her team to determine whom I would put in charge when she inevitably failed her task. And she would. It was evident in her demeanor she thought I was beneath her. Not only that, her attitude made it obvious she didn't care about her position here. What she did have an interest in was Stone.

At my desk, I read through resumes and performance evaluations. The other two designers were competent, but one stood out. Delilah. She managed most of the complicated tasks and designs. Not only that, she stayed considerably longer than the rest to get things done to meet deadlines. I shot off a quick email to her to meet with me in a half hour.

It would be interesting if Delilah told Celia who she was meeting with. My guess was she was smart enough to keep her own counsel where Celia was concerned.

"Adeline."

Stone's voice sent a jolt of heat through me, and I stood on legs that wobbled. Why that man affected me like that… I steeled myself to focus on the job and went into his office with my iPad in hand. "Yes?"

My mind momentarily blanked at the sight of him behind

his desk. He had on a charcoal suit that stretched across his broad shoulders, white button-down, and black tie. His hair was disheveled like he'd run his fingers through it, and his intense onyx gaze held a flame that licked over every inch of me. I swallowed back a sigh, and after a slow blink to re-center, tilted my chin up a notch.

"Why is Celia emailing me and complaining?"

"I'm handling it." She would throw a fit, though, and I had to make sure he was still uninterested in the small details. "Just to clarify, you don't want any contact with the design crew. I'm free to manage them?"

"Yes. All I care about is the design is executed to maintain the original old-world ambiance from the nineteenth century that fits well with Verona."

"Great. And so that you're aware, I plan to shift the lead in the team."

"Fine. Where is the San Francisco report?"

"I'll forward it to you." I clicked through the files on my device and sent it through. "Your schedule is updated, the board meeting confirmed and moved back an hour. I have three documents that need your signature. They're in your task folders, lined up in order of importance. Is there anything else you need?"

He leaned back in his chair, a small smile curving his kissable lips. Where had that thought come from? I straightened my spine and thought about the pending confrontation as a distraction.

"Tiffany thought I should take it easy on you this week, but you don't seem to have any problem managing the workload."

I loved challenges, and his workload fed my thirst for problem-solving. "No. If you need anything else taken off your plate, I have time."

"I have several properties I'm thinking of buying. I'd like you to research them and get back to me with an analysis."

"Of course." I backed out of his office as the phone rang at my desk. Delilah walked in, and I waved to the couch on the side of the suite near the large windows. After transferring the expected call to Stone, I introduced myself. "I've gone over your employee file and see that you've worked for Stone Enterprises for the past five years."

With jean-clad legs crossed, she nervously bobbed her foot while twisting her hands in her lap. "Yes. That's correct."

"And when Sally resigned, you were offered Celia's position but declined?"

"I didn't feel ready. I—I don't have any formal training."

"You have talent and dedication." In the five minutes I took looking through her portfolio that was on record, her skill was crystal clear. "I'd like to move you up to team lead, should an opening arise." I leaned back and smiled, hoping to set her at ease.

"I don't think—"

"Delilah, don't worry about not having the schooling. That's not what I'm looking for, and Mr. Crenshaw will back me up on this. The question of when your promotion will happen is merely due to timing. I wanted to talk with you about it first."

"Oh okay." She cleared her throat. "Thank you."

"You're very welcome." I rose, signaling our chat was over. As we walked to the elevator, I placed my hand on her shoulder. "I don't want you to worry. You wouldn't be on your own. I'd be willing to help you with ordering or anything you need until you're comfortable. We'll probably implement the process in steps. For now, Delilah, let's keep our little chat about your future between us."

Understanding shone in her light-brown eyes, and she nodded.

My cell pinged, and a glance showed it was from Eileen. She was traveling through France then Spain and had sent several pictures. I sent a text commenting and telling her I missed her and that I'd call soon. After sending the text, my finger hovered over my contacts. I brought up Tommy and unblocked him. My phone flooded with unread messages, and my intent to answer was swept aside by the sheer magnitude of responding. I'd do it after work.

I set my cell on my desk. Five minutes passed since Delilah had left and I'd pulled up the properties Stone wanted an analysis on when Celia stormed in. The angry click of her absurdly high Jimmy Choos stopped when she halted in front of my desk. I scrolled through electronic faxes from her department, checking for a revised purchase order. Of course, she could've handled it over the phone.

My cell pinged, flashing Tommy's name. Celia leaned toward it, the text message easy to see. I pressed my lips together as his texts lit up my locked screen. I cupped the phone and slipped it into one of the drawers, out of sight from her prying eyes.

"Who's Tommy?"

"Thank you for being prompt, Celia." I kept my voice neutral, my words brief.

"The handles are already being installed—"

"Which ones?" I had to make sure.

Defiance flashed across her features, evident in the devious tilt to her very red lips. "The brushed nickel."

I ignored her and punched in the number for the foreman. "Steve, Adeline here." After a quick greeting, I got to the point. "Please uninstall all the brushed nickel handles and box them for return."

Celia crossed her arms and sneered. "Wait until Stone—"

"Mr. Crenshaw," I cut her off. They knew each other, had some kind of history. Even so, I couldn't let her have the upper hand. Besides, I knew he could hear her shrill voice.

Celia's lips pursed. "It's humorous."

I shouldn't do this but did. Making sure my tone sounded as tired of the conversation as I was, I asked, "What is?"

"You, with your silly aspirations of power. Thinking you have an eye for design when you wear cheap clothes, gaudy makeup, knockoff bags, and shoes with scuff marks. Once *Stone* hears of this—"

"I've heard all I need to." Stone pushed off his doorjamb and moved to my side. "I'm well aware that your uncle is on the board, and out of respect for him, I've put up with your bullshit. But if you want to keep your job, then you'll recognize that Adeline's position is above yours. She is the one you answer to. Stop involving me with your petty problems. Do as Adeline said and fix the design issue. She knows what I want done."

Celia huffed then twirled on her heels—without falling— and exited our office penthouse. I leaned back in my chair, crossing my arms. There could be an issue with demoting her. "Uncle on the board?"

"Yes. Celia is here as a favor to him."

"She doesn't seem to want to do the work, though. I'm confused why she's here."

"My guess is she wants to land a wealthy husband." He pulled his wallet from his pants and withdrew a black credit card. "This has nothing to do with what Celia said, but you'll need clothes for this weekend, specifically for dinner with the Mariucci's."

I pinched the metal unlimited-spending credit card between my fingertips. I held my head high, refusing to feel bad for being poor. "This contradicts what you're saying."

"Just buy some damn clothes, Adeline." He ran his hand through his hair, frustration evident around the tiny lines bracketing his mouth. "Yours are fine, but as my fiancée, they'll expect you to have a wardrobe that my income would allow for."

"Fine." I tucked the card in my purse. This was part of the contract and him getting what he wanted—the Bianca. I could compartmentalize it that way, rather than taking it as an insult to my situation.

Stone frowned. "I meant what I said." His gaze traveled over my crossed legs. "I like how you dress."

Heat flooded my cheeks, and I ducked my head, intent to get back to work, not letting my mind dwell on that he liked my formfitting pants. I had more pressing matters. "Will her uncle be a problem should I demote Celia?" What I wanted to ask was, would she?

"I'll handle it."

THE PHONE RANG TWICE BEFORE EILEEN ANSWERED. I DIDN'T even let her speak—just jumped right into the mess I feared I was making of things. "Eileen, I wish you were here."

"What's wrong?" Alarm infused her voice, raising it an entire octave.

I flopped onto my back on my bed and glanced out the window of my bedroom while dusk painted the view with red and orange sunset hues and lengthening shadows. "Everything. I don't know what's going on with me. I'm doing things that are so completely uncharacteristic. I mean, the way I acted in this meeting Stone and I went to. It was—"

"Wait, what? Stone? You're on first-name basis?"

I cringed. "It's a long story."

"Lucky for you, I have plenty of time."

The smile in her voice came through loud and clear, and I sighed. This was why I called. She would be able to talk me off the ledge. In an abbreviated version, I filled my best friend in about the coveted hotel Stone wanted and the obstacle that he saw in his way of achieving it. As well as his solution to even the playing field—me. I confessed about the credit card and my shopping trip before I had called her. When I got to the way I behaved in the meeting with Mr. Mariucci, she burst out laughing.

"I can't believe you said Satan's Mistress. Wow, I wish I'd been there."

"You would have snorted Pellegrino and taken the heat from me."

"That I would." She giggled.

I could picture her lounging across her bed, too, talking to me like we had when we were roommates not long ago. "This is so out of hand, Eileen. It's like I'm possessed. I mean, I'm so bold with him. And this is my ticket to a secure future. I don't understand what's going on. I've never behaved like this."

"Addy—"

"Don't start." She called me that nickname when she was about to unload a whole lot of stuff I didn't want to hear. It was why I called her, but…

"It's clear you were staking a claim, defending him, at the meeting."

"No way. You know I don't behave unprofessionally when it comes to anything involving my career, my goals."

"Yeah, I get that. But this is different. You didn't act like this with Tommy. Ever. I swear he was more like your big brother than an on-again off-again boyfriend."

"He texted me. I haven't answered him yet."

"That's a separate conversation." Eileen huffed. "What's going on here is that you like your boss."

The attraction I felt every time he was near burned like a brand in my mind. She was right. I just wasn't ready to admit it for a very good reason. "I can't. You know I need this job."

"It'll be okay. Let yourself enjoy this. You'll never know if you missed out on something if you don't."

I understood what she was saying, but allowing the feelings I had for him could ruin everything.

CHAPTER 7

ADELINE

Decadent silk from my new dress swirled around my thighs with each step as I linked my arm in Stone's. There was something magical about Venice. While we walked to the Riviera to meet Vince and Margaret Mariucci for dinner, I soaked up the romantic moodiness of the old-world buildings that saturated the floating city with their stunning architecture and history.

The island didn't allow cars, and after a water taxi, we walked, passing other couples and individuals along the way. We had already checked in at the Bianca's front desk and collected the keycards for our room—singular—and they assured us our bags would be brought up. I wasn't sure how I felt about sharing a room with Stone.

Preoccupied with our sleeping arrangements, my heel caught on a brick in the street, and my ankle buckled. "Oww," I cried out as I fell against him—*stupid heels*.

Stone's arm slipped around my waist, tethering me to his side as we crossed over a small bridge that connected to more charming but narrow streets. "You're a little accident-prone, aren't you?"

"Truth's out." I relaxed, letting him maintain my balance on these stilts. He could handle it, especially since he was so tall, which made me feel like a doll beside him. "I was more of a tomboy growing up. Heels aren't my thing." I glanced down at them. "Even if they are pretty."

"Hmm. I pegged you as a girly-girl."

His behavior changed as soon as we'd left Verona. Almost playful, and dare I say flirty? For the millionth time, I snuck a peek at him, unused to his much-improved attitude. We neared the restaurant, and I almost sighed with the prospect of getting off my feet.

Brushing my curiosity away, I addressed his disbelief of how I'd been when younger. "I used to throw around a football with my neighbor all the time. Looks can be deceiving. The fact that I have a brain seems to shock people too."

Stone barked out a laugh, and I fought a shiver as his body hummed with mirth against mine. "I assumed as much since Tiffany hired you. She wouldn't have let anyone in the door who couldn't competently keep up with the workload, and I would have fired you."

"Ahh, then you could have promoted Celia to work alongside you and fulfilled half of her dream."

He grunted. "That would never happen. Is she giving you a hard time?"

I shrugged, or tried to, while squished between his arm and side. "She tries. I'll give her that. But I've got a plan to manage her, so long as I can fire her if needed?"

"I'll deal with her uncle. He'll understand, if she's given the proper warning and write-ups."

"Of course. The door handle instance was the first. I expect a few more, and then I can move Delilah into Celia's position."

We spotted Vince and Margaret seated at a waterfront table and made our way over to them. Stone released me as I stepped forward to shake both of their hands. After he did the same, he pulled out my seat. With a glance over my shoulder, I winked at him. A girl could get used to having someone as dreamy as him wait on her hand and foot.

Once Stone was seated, and we placed our drink orders, Margaret turned to me. Her deep-brown eyes sparkled. Older by maybe thirty years, she was still movie-star beautiful, with a genuine warmth that radiated from her. I liked her immediately.

"I've looked forward to meeting you both. And you'll be here all weekend?"

"Just for the night," Stone answered.

Nope, that wasn't going to work for me. I stretched my proverbial contract-granted power as his fake fiancée. "I've already cleared your schedule, honey." I met Margaret's gaze with a huge grin. "We most definitely will be staying the entire weekend. There is so much to see and do." I patted his arm as he narrowed his eyes at me. "You'll be glad we did." I barely withheld my chuckle at blindsiding him.

Margaret laughed conspiratorially. "That's the way to do it. Otherwise, we'd never spend time with our men."

"Don't I know it." I thanked the waiter as he handed me a menu while catching the concerned pinch to Stone's features before he wiped the expression from his face. "I have big plans for us. Starting with St. Mark's Basilica, lunch in the piazza, and then take a gondola ride on the Canale Grande. Oh, we can't miss the Gallerie dell'Accademia either."

"Don't forget Doges Palace, and you must cross over the Bridge of Sighs too," Margaret added. "As for lunch, I'd recommend eating at Osteria All'Arco. It's well-known by locals and is standing room only, unless you're able to snag one of the seats on the small terrace." Her features softened, and she gifted her husband with a blinding smile. "It's our favorite place to go together."

"That sounds lovely. We definitely will." I couldn't wait for tomorrow. I'd never left my hometown, and this was my chance to experience Venice, in addition to Verona. It wouldn't be the first place I would travel to either. I'd make sure of that by having a well-paying, stable career.

The waiter returned a few minutes later, and Stone looked to me.

"I couldn't decide. I'm so hungry I could eat everything they've got." I hated relying on him, but I was overwhelmed at the moment. "Would you order for me, please?" *Oh, wait…* I narrowed my eyes on him, aware I probably wasn't like the women he usually dated. "*Not* a salad."

With a raised eyebrow and the corners of his lips twitching, he rattled off several dishes to the waiter. I didn't pay attention as I stole peeks at the tables around us. Their meals consisted of gourmet, pleasing-to-the-eye dishes, but for my appetite, small on the plate.

Once the orders were taken care of, Stone and Vince chatted about another hotel chain that had fallen into trouble and their thoughts about combining efforts and rescuing the European branch. I half-listened, interested that Stone had proposed going into business together for a project. From what I'd read, he didn't take on business partners. Something about the Mariuccis must appeal to him.

I tapped my nail and wracked my brain about what to talk to Margaret about, doing my best to ignore the guys, even though I wanted to offer an opinion. "Stone tells me you have two children?"

"Grown." She positively glowed. "Our oldest daughter has a two-year-old son and is due any day with a baby girl. Vince and I would like to slow down so we can enjoy our grand-children and do some traveling too."

My thoughts turned to my parents and all they were never able to do and how it seemed as if their dreams died with them. "You should do it. Life is short, and each day you're together matters."

"You sound like you speak from experience." She reached out and squeezed my hand.

With my other, I took a fortifying sip of my wine. "My parents passed away before they could do the traveling they always talked about. They would have when I went away to college, but my mom left us long before then, and my dad lost the will to do anything without her. He wouldn't stray too far from me either. He worried. I wished he hadn't." I shrugged. This was going deep, but opening myself up to her wouldn't hurt Stone. If anything, I had a feeling this would sway Margaret more in our favor, and in turn, Vince. "He died during my fourth year at university with anxiety over how I'd be taken care of." It was unnecessary; he knew I could take care of myself. But he was old-fashioned and wanted to see me settled to ease his conscience.

"I'm so sorry." She dabbed at the corner of her eye. "I take it he hadn't met Stone, or I'm sure he wouldn't have been as concerned about your future."

I waved that thought away with a grin. "We weren't dating then, but he shouldn't have had a single concern. I'm more than capable of taking care of myself. Meeting Stone was…" I paused because this part was something I didn't even like admitting to myself and too close to the truth. "Unexpected. Yet like running into someone I'd known my entire life. Weird, I know, but there's this connection, attraction, I can't deny." Stone was mid-sip when he choked. Guess he was listening. I patted his back then took a deep breath. I'd come this far, may as well say the last thing on my mind. "I've never felt this way with anyone else."

"Well, I think you're good for him. I've run into Stone a time or two during functions I've attended with Vince, and he always struck me as very driven. Not a bad thing, but you balance that with fun, injecting a little spontaneity into his workaholic world." Her hand rested on Vince's arm. "It's something I do for Vince as well."

"I hope you don't mind me asking, but your children don't want to get into the family business?" I sensed rather than felt Stone's focused attention beside me.

"Sadly, no. Our son went into the military and is making a career out of it. Our daughter doesn't have a head for the hotel business and instead went into fashion design. She is doing that in her spare time while she stays home with her son and the new one soon to be born. With the sale of the Bianca, we plan to add to their trust funds and our grand-kids' college accounts."

"That's lovely. It's wonderful that you don't put pressure on them to take over your legacy if they don't want to."

Our food arrived, and we fell silent for a few minutes. Stone had selected several side dishes as well as our main ones, and I enjoyed the decadent tastes. I kept eyeing Stone's grilled mackerel until he held a forkful for me to try. Holy crap, each plate was just as wonderful, if not better, than the last. My eyes rolled back in my head at the flavors. I tasted my dish again. So good, but I wanted his. I narrowed my eyes until he swapped our plates.

"My mistake." He grinned. "I should have ordered double."

"Yes, you should have." I'd tried, but I couldn't leave it alone. "Vince, I overheard you talking about hotelier Arnold Pierce and his feud with his business partner. It's a shame the Grande Victorian is in jeopardy. Pierce claimed bankruptcy and fled the country, correct?"

"He did. Leaving Nick Reynolds as sole owner. From my understanding, he's trying to renegotiate the loans and save the hotel."

"I read an article that Nick has original artwork from Pablo Picasso and Amedeo Modigilani that he inherited from his great grandfather. Should you and Stone decide to partner with him, you could do something with the art. Change the scope of the hotel so that there are private viewings available to the guests in a secure room, possibly with a dining experience? There could be other avenues to explore there as well. But definitely upscale."

Vince's brows arched high on his forehead, and Stone chuckled. "She's a surprise, isn't she? Should we decide to enter into business with Nick, we'll have Adeline execute her vision. What she comes up with turns to gold."

While Stone and Vince hashed out possibilities, Margaret and I chatted about the artists who originated from Venice. Dinner flew by, and before I knew it, we were heading back to our room. Fog rolled in, making the narrow alleyways dangerous for those who didn't know their way. A few ended on water. To step off the path into murky depths didn't hold appeal, even if there was an eerie romantic quality to the hazy mist. I was glad for the sureness of our hosts and the assurance that Stone wouldn't let anything happen to me.

"I love that restaurant," I said to Vince and Margaret as we walked to the hotel. Stone's hand settled on my hip, pulling me tight to his side.

"It's one of our favorites," Vince said as Margaret hugged me. He and Stone shook hands, and we said goodnight and then stepped into the elevator.

"We'll have to do this again," Stone said.

"Definitely." Vince's grin stretched even farther.

I moved to put some space between Stone and me, the buzzing awareness every time I was close to him—or he touched me—messing with my head. While the evening had been wonderful, what was between us was a farce, and I needed to keep my emotions and reactions to him in check when we were alone.

After the elevator doors closed, he glanced at my

discarded heels. A brow raised in amusement. "Do you think that's a good idea?"

His deep voice sent goose bumps dancing over my bare skin. I bent and picked them up, letting the shoes dangle from my fingertips. "No one's watching us."

"Hmm."

I narrowed my gaze; those noncommittal answers of his drove me crazy. "The dinner went well. I think your chance of winning the contract is significantly higher than George and Anne Fielding."

"Thanks to you." The elevator doors opened, and he ushered me into the hallway with a hand on the small of my back. Pretty sconces were spaced along the walls, softly lighting our way.

"It's beautiful here."

Stone pushed open our door, and I stepped inside to walls decorated in neutral tans with an exquisite handwoven oriental rug covering most of the hardwood floor. A plush loveseat faced its twin, making up an inviting sitting area. I swept my gaze around the room that touched on old-world elegance with exquisite paintings until alarm shot through. "Wait. Why is there only one door leading off this room?" Please be two beds… I could handle that better than having to share. I didn't think either one of us would be comfortable sleeping on anything in the living room.

Stone loosened his tie and unbuttoned the top button of his shirt. "It's not ideal, but we are trying to convince them we're engaged. What do you think two beds, or an adjoining room, would have told them?"

I tilted my head to the side. He had a point. It didn't mean I was happy about sleeping in the same bed with my boss.

With determination, I swept past him into the bedroom. A king-size poster bed greeted me. That was all I could see, not the dressers or the gauzy curtains. *I can do this.* With renewed purpose, I went to the dresser, seeing that the hotel staff unpacked my bag.

Scanning which graphic tee fit my mood, I grabbed it and sleep shorts, stomping to the bathroom first, an evil glare thrown his way for good measure. *One bed?* Door shut and locked, I brushed my teeth and cursed him some more. Who would've known if we had two queens? Or better yet, a full suite with two bedrooms?

Face washed and my PJ's on, I left my little sanctuary to find him pulling his shoes off. His tie was missing, and several buttons were undone on his shirt, exposing taut skin and… my mouth dropped open. Then my fingers twitched, desperate to run over all those forbidden muscles flexing as he stood.

"We need to set some ground rules." More for me—the goal was too important. I couldn't complicate whatever this was by messing around with my boss.

A too enticing, crooked grin curved his kissable lips as he read my T-shirt. I shook my head. Focus!

"I see you're wearing the rules?"

I nodded. That was why I picked this shirt. My love of graphic tees was vast. I had a saying for every possible mood I could have. This one said: Nope, not today. That rule was good enough for now. I couldn't come up with anything more. Stone, out of his shirt, muddled my cognitive abilities. I got into bed, turned my back on him, and willed myself to sleep.

Five minutes later, the dip in the mattress sent a fresh surge of alarm through my veins, and my body shifted toward him. Scrambling back to my spot, I lay there, frozen. When nothing happened, I relaxed a little. Nothing would happen. I almost snorted at what this was—my reactions to him, not his to me. He wasn't interested in me. I was seriously delusional.

CHAPTER 8

ADELINE

My eyes popped open, and I went from a deep sleep to reluctantly awake and groggy. Something was different. My body was on fire, and the mattress was hard beneath me, not soft as I'd thought. Aside from the discomfort to find the bathroom, I didn't want to get up. Seconds ticked by and reality seeped into my consciousness, and in its wake, a rush of panic.

Not the mattress—I was sprawled across Stone.

Notmylifenotmylife.

Please be asleep. My left leg entwined between his, and I was lying over his bare chest. My face burned in mortification. I was violating my own rule, the one I had printed on my T-shirt: nope, not today. Ugh. Maybe not last night, but apparently, my body interpreted the message that this morning was fair game.

For a few seconds, I studied his features. Lashes too long to be fair dusted over his cheeks. My gaze explored from his sleep-mussed hair to his very kissable, dangerous lips. With a slow blink, I steeled myself to make my escape. Being this close to him was messing with my resolve, and that was another humiliation I couldn't face—his rejection and my sure-to-follow tanked career.

I inched off him while fighting the urge to explore the ridges and valleys of his chest. My arms shook as I pushed up and eased back, taking care not to make any sudden movements. Because I didn't think I would live down the embarrassment. And they were wracking up. I spilled coffee on his desk, then I tripped and face-planted onto his crotch, and now this?

When my feet were on the floor, I hightailed it into the bathroom. After a quick shower, I yanked on a pair of yoga pants and another graphic tee. As I snuck from our room in search of coffee, I took in the empty bed. He was awake.

Pulling up my proverbial big-girl panties, I left the bedroom to face Stone. Hopefully, he didn't have a clue that I'd used him for a full-body pillow throughout the night.

The intoxicating scent of coffee lured me to the dining table like a siren's song, and right to where Stone worked on his laptop. Not ready to see the look on his face, I ducked my head, so my hair curtained around my face, then grunted "morning."

His response was distracted, and some of the utter embarrassment faded. I poured myself a generous cup of coffee and snagged a pastry from a huge array of food. Oh, God, there was so much. My brain short-circuited from the sensory overload of the many choices spread out on the table, and my mouth watered. There was scrambled eggs, toast, and *bacon*—my focus went there. I wiped beneath my mouth, making sure the drool was imaginary. Nothing else mattered until I got my hands on that. I prepared to eat my weight in food. Because—have an emotion, will eat.

I filled a plate to overflowing and plopped down across from him. His gaze flicked up, and after a second, his lips twitched. I rolled my eyes. "Go ahead. Out with whatever's amusing." My hair was washed and not a giant rat's nest anymore, so it couldn't be that.

"Two things."

I huffed, secretly hoping it wasn't about how I'd invaded his personal space while sleeping. May as well continue to shovel bacon in my mouth while waiting to hear something else that would inflame my face.

"Your T-shirt."

I glanced down to double-check which one I'd worn. Yep, that was the one I wanted; it fit my mood. It said: Never trust an atom. They make up everything.

"And the sheer amount of food you eat while you look like you weigh about a hundred pounds."

I shrugged. "Fast metabolism. My mom was the same way."

He shook his head as a chime from an incoming email sounded. His focus shifted, and I went back to the bacon. I wouldn't let his workaholic tendencies deter me from finishing my breakfast.

Mission accomplished and stomach full, I leaned back, took sips of my second cup of life-giving coffee, and let my gaze wander over his messed-up hair and rumpled dress shirt from last night. My fingers drummed on the top of the table while I alternated from looking at him and the windows. If we stayed in this room, there was a much better way to spend the time than glued to a laptop. *And on that note.* "When are we heading out to explore Venice?"

"*We* aren't. I have a lot of work to do, but you can."

That wasn't going to work for me. "If Vince or Margaret find out we stayed in the hotel room all day after we told them we would be exploring, it wouldn't look great. It would make us liars, and we don't want to alert them to that fact so early, do we?"

"I didn't say I was going to do any of those sightseeing things. You did."

"Doesn't matter. They think we both will, and it doesn't show a promising side to our relationship if we aren't arm-in-arm and exploring the city. And we have a contract—I won't let you sabotage my efforts by staying in." I motioned for the computer. "Why don't you go shower, and I'll work on whatever it is you need done?"

His brow rose, and a speculative gleam flashed in his eyes. That was better than the partial ignoring he'd been doing.

"I'm working my way through the tasks. I'll agree to sightseeing today, but I need to head back tonight. We're not staying the whole weekend." He swung the laptop around so I could see the long list of things he had planned to get done. "Have at it."

Oh, I would. As soon as he stood from the table, I got to work, excited about my win. I read the partial response he'd typed to one of his employees. It was good. I liked how his brain worked; he was smart, fast, and efficient. But so was I, and we could knock this work out together in no time at all.

It didn't take long for Stone to get ready, and I filled him in on the progress I'd made to his workload. We would put another hour or two in on the way back to Verona. I swapped out my graphic tee for a sundress, and we left the room. In keeping with what I wanted to see, we agreed to visit Doge's Palace as our first stop, thankful for the tickets Margaret had managed to get to us before we left. They were waiting at the hotel's reservation desk and would allow us to bypass the huge line to get into the palace.

I'd planned for us to take a gondola ride back to the Bianca later so we could pack and check out. After arriving via water taxi, we strolled through the city while weaving amidst the throngs of tourists. Stone pointed out bits of history along the way, and I fell deeper in love with the city of bridges.

We purchased a snack as we neared our first stop. Our hands brushed against each other as we traveled through the narrow street, and finally, we threaded our fingers together as we'd awkwardly done in the hotel. After doing so several times already, the move felt natural, familiar. When we came across Doge's Palace, I stopped in my tracks. Stone let go of my hand and instead slipped his arm around my waist. I leaned against him while taking in the sheer artwork that was the palace. Symbolism of strength, justice, prayer, and government wove through the sculptures and beautifully designed façade.

Once inside, we wandered through the museum, admiring the artwork explicitly crafted for the building. As we walked, Stone and I discussed the various movements and how the styles changed with the influence of the time period. I shared my love of impressionism and artists like Claude Monet. We debated the different schools from expressionism to abstract and how neither of us was too fond of some of them aside from a select few artist. Where we found common ground was in photorealism and realism. Excitement thrummed through me with each new point he brought up or countered, and I couldn't stop smiling over how much fun I was having. Time ceased to matter while we strolled hand in hand through famous exhibits, and I didn't want it to end.

I could have spent an entire day here, but there would be other opportunities. We exited the palace on the Grande Canal side and stepped onto the Bridge of Sighs. The corridor connected to the first floor of the prison. In the passage, our steps slowed, and I mulled over Stone's aversion to the lower level at the Verona hotel. "I get the impression you want out of Hotel Destino, that it's not your favorite project."

My sundress swirled around my legs as we paused near the middle of the Bridge of Sighs and leaned against the stone. One of the windows offered a view of the canal below us. The passage was busy, and people moved around us in the tight corridor.

A gondola passed beneath the bridge, and I couldn't help the small smile at the sight, despite the heavy weight of despair that clung to the stones within the walls. The thought that those who had crossed this bridge so many years ago would never experience the beauty of Venice again as they parted from their love ones to endure the finality of prison, and often the end of their lives, was crushing. The sense of loss warred with the romance of the floating island, and sadness seeped into my bones. Before I sunk too low, Stone's voice startled me back to the present as he answered my previous question.

"The hotel in Venice is different. I had a compulsion to buy the one in Verona. For years after a trip to Italy, I couldn't stop thinking about Hotel Destino. Then one day, I heard rumors the owner was contemplating selling. That was my chance." A breeze ruffled his dark hair, and I half-turned, riveted by the faraway look that settled over his features. "I didn't expect to feel the way I do onsite. The longer I'm there, the worse I sleep, and the more I'm unsettled."

He fell silent, and I wasn't sure if I should interject, but I wanted to understand what he meant because I, too, felt a pull to the hotel. With a tap of my fingers against the stone, I dug deeper with my questions. "And last night? Did you sleep well, or were you still tied to the urgency driving you to complete the Verona project?"

A wolfish grin curved his lips as he leaned forward to

peer through one of the tiny windows, his body partially turned toward me. "Best night I've had in a long time."

I pressed my lips together to stop from blurting anything inappropriate. The sensation of his solid body beneath mine when I woke flooded my mind, and I could think of little else. If only I could call my friend, Eileen, and confide in her right now. I knew what she'd tell me to do. She'd say go for it. But my future… Would crossing the line like we had compromise my career goals? That was the only thing that truly held me back.

"So, no bad dreams here?" There was something about that hotel in Verona. I was simultaneously drawn and repelled to it. His description matched my feelings.

"Not a one. Which brings me to a needed amendment to our contract."

My spine straightened, and I mirrored his stance, so we were both facing one another. I had a suspicion about where his thought process would lead based on his relaxed attitude. Venice was good for him, Verona, not so much.

"I got a call early this morning that a pipe burst while the construction crew was working. You'll have to move into another room temporarily. I think it should be my suite as none of the other rooms have been furnished yet. I have a spare bedroom, and we can get a lot more accomplished workwise to get the hell out of the Verona project."

"Oh okay. I guess." But for good? There was something bittersweet about the hotel. I couldn't see not wanting to return now and again. Regardless, I couldn't fault his reasoning for moving to a room of my own in his suite as it seemed to be strictly work-related. Besides, I didn't think he felt the same as me. Aside from a few glances here and there, I wasn't sure if he was as attracted to me as I was to him, although there were moments where his actions confused me.

He tucked a piece of hair behind my ear, and I caught myself before swaying forward as his fingers trailed along the curve of my jaw before falling away. *Like that!* That was not a professional gesture, and the Mariuccis were nowhere in sight. The thought of sharing space with him in the evenings held an appeal I couldn't refuse. I wasn't able to fight the pull I felt toward him, nor did I think I wanted to.

"I won't lose this deal, Adeline. The faster the Venice acquisition goes, the sooner we can move here and get started on a new project. The Verona hotel will wrap up without us needing to be onsite. Soon, we'll be out of there. For good."

I jolted back a step. "You don't want to return there, even to see how the hotel is running?"

"No. That's why I have managers in place that I trust. Tiffany will eventually be back. I may stop in once in a while, but I will never stay over there again."

His skin was pulled taut with eyes that seemed haunted. I couldn't fight my reaction and went with my gut, stepping into his arms and resting my cheek on his chest to offer comfort. In his embrace, I felt safe. Something I didn't realize was missing from my life after my parents passed away.

He tugged on the ends of my hair. "Come on. Let's get some lunch."

As his arms fell away, his fingers threaded with mine, something we did unconsciously more often than not. In a daze, I walked beside Stone, letting him guide me through the bridge's tight corridor and back to Doge's Palace rather than to the prison that connected on the other side. I wanted to explore more, but I had a feeling there would be time to do so in the future.

Before I knew it, we were at an outdoor table on the small terrace, the restaurant Margaret had recommended. I waited while he went inside to order for us. The restaurant was busy, and we'd gotten lucky snagging this table as another couple stood to leave.

The dreams that plagued Stone, and my vision when I arrived at the hotel, swirled in my brain. The name the psychic at our sorority bash told me about came to mind, and I did a quick internet search on my phone to see what I could come up with concerning the Verona hotel. There had to be a connection. I felt it deep in my bones.

After several minutes, I found what I was looking for. Only, I'd thought he would still be alive. The medium failed to mention he was not.

Cristiano Santoro, bellhop, and son of Sergio Santoro, who was the doorman for the Hotel Destino, existed in the nineteenth century. There was even a picture of the staff. It was old, dated. The photo's age was evident even on the internet: sepia and granular. My heart slammed against my rib cage. There was something familiar about Cristiano.

Then I recognized what. It was in his jawline, wolfish grin, broad shoulders, and intensity that consumed the space he occupied that reminded me of Stone.

CHAPTER 9

STONE

usk replaced the brilliant sunlight from earlier. The lingering rays shrunk as they faded, clinging to the wood floor in my office in Verona. I had a headache and wasn't in the mood to play referee as Leif droned on over our scheduled call about having to collaborate with Brenda to get the quarterly reports done. I was tired of hearing excuses. Not only that, my mind kept wandering to Adeline. The way she lit up a room with her smile, the jolt of electricity that followed a simple brush of her hand, and how well we worked and played together. I wanted more and puzzled over how to make that happen.

She postponed moving her things to my suite as we'd got in to Verona late last night. Tonight, she'd be there and my blood heated at the thought of her so near, my mind wanting to wander to what that would be like.

But for the moment, I had to get through this conversation with Leif, my usually competent employee. As his voice registered once more, the ache at my temples ratcheted up another notch. Would this day never end? At the very least, I needed to put an end to this call and cut off his excuses. "Handle it, Leif."

Disconnecting, I ran my hands over my face, willing the exhaustion to go away. I hated this hotel. Failure and sadness oozed from its tired walls, and I feared that no amount of interior design refresh would expel the stench of it.

"Adeline."

The scent of summer and lilies arrived half a second before she did. The pain behind my eyes eased as she drew closer. Maybe I was getting sick. "I'm leaving for the board meeting and need you to handle overseeing new designs for the basement." Just saying it left a bitter taste in my mouth, but there was no way I could deal with Celia.

Adeline cocked her head, and I wished her hair was down. It would have spilled in a silky fall of silvery blonde over her shoulder and down her arm. The need to touch her brought me to my feet. The chair rolled a few inches as I stood. I rounded the desk, and I took her hand in mine, toying with the engagement ring she'd taken to wearing—even at the office.

As if a thread connected us, she took a half step forward, and the stress of the day diminished. For the first time in years, I wanted to skip the meeting and explore the city with her instead. I had yet to visit Juliet's Wall, an iconic site in Verona.

There was something about being with Adeline that screamed of destiny, if I believed in that. My gaze fell to her full lips as they shaped unheard words that slowly filtered back into my brain. Yep, I had to be coming down with something. I shook off the spell I seemed to be under in her presence and concentrated on what she was saying.

"What were you thinking of for the basement rooms? From what I'd seen of the plans, we were to mimic the first floor."

With effort, I kept my face neutral, fighting the need to frown at the feelings of failure and loss at the mention of the lower level. "I changed my mind. I want the space to rival the penthouse suites, so when guests stay there, the amenities and luxury supersede being underground. Play with the idea of tearing down some of the walls to create a luxury apartment-like atmosphere."

Her brow creased with delicate worry lines, and she pressed the back of her hand to my forehead. "Are you all right?"

My fingers stilled on hers, and I fought the urge to pull her into my arms. We'd gotten accustomed to touching each other last weekend in Venice. She affected me far more than I wanted to admit to myself. "Just a headache. I'll grab food on my way to the meeting. I'm sure that's all it is."

"Okay." She pursed her lips. "Are there designs for the basement then? Or are you trusting the crew to come up with something?"

Not likely. "No finalized plans and I don't trust Celia's take on this project. You'll need to head it up with either her or one of the other members of the team. Bring me the preliminary ideas once they come up with them, and I'll look over them." I stepped away then thought better of it, shifting back to hold her gaze. I'd crossed the line with us at the mention of her being my fake fiancée. I wanted more, needed it. "We'll go over them tonight at dinner."

What I was about to do would be the next step in solidifying more with her.

Adeline

Worry shadowed my every move as I drew closer to meeting with Celia. I didn't like how exhausted Stone looked. The annoyance in his voice when he'd spoken to Leif was something I could help him with. I'd chatted with Leif a few times already and understood what he expected of his staff. It helped that I had a ton of experience working for, and anticipating the needs of, others during high school and college. Brenda was a recent hire and reported to Leif. I'd talked to her a few times on the phone and made a note on my daily tasks for today to coach her a bit on what to expect and the best way to communicate with her boss.

The elevator dinged, and I stepped off and into the reception area. Construction workers moved about carrying in the new flooring to lay tomorrow. We'd salvaged as much as possible, but there were sections that were beyond our craftsman's ability to bring back to life. And the lobby centerpiece was scheduled to arrive within the hour.

I swung my gaze from where the men worked in search of the design team. Delilah and Betty stood with heads bent together before the reception counter plans spread out before them, and fabric swatches piled haphazardly at their elbows. And then there was Celia, nail file in hand as she chatted on her Bluetooth. That better be a vendor she was talking to. I moved to confront her but bounced off of Steve, our foreman, who steadied me with a hand at my elbow.

"Are you all right, Adeline?" His gravelly voice brought a smile to my face.

"I'm good. Sorry about that. I wasn't watching where I was going." The few times we'd spoken had endeared him to me. There was no pushback. He didn't make me feel inferior or lesser just because I was young and a woman. He was fair and got the work done without complaint or excuses. And I liked how he treated his team. Plus, we both struggled to deal with the shit show that was Celia.

"I meant to call you. We unloaded the artwork ordered for the lobby. There were a few additional boxes. You may want to check in with…" He rubbed the back of his neck and grimaced. "Celia."

"Will do." I gave him a tight-lipped smile in anticipation of the confrontation that was sure to follow the lower-level discussion. As I walked away, I paused, then turned back. That task could propel the changes that would inevitably happen. "Steve, where are the boxes?"

With a wary eye, he pointed me in the right direction. Avoiding Celia for the moment, I went directly to the cluster of crates. Delilah noticed me right away, and we nodded to one another, but she didn't approach me. I could guess why by the resigned expression on hers and Betty's faces. It seems they knew what would go down when I looked at the order.

The crates with the paintings were already opened, and I peeked inside. One of Steve's workers came over and helped me to lift one of them to get a better look. My breath caught in my throat. Sweeping strokes captured the Italian landscape as the sun crested the horizon, chasing the fog away. This set the tone when guests first arrived beautifully, and to be honest, I was surprised Celia hadn't screwed the purchase up somehow, adding her love of all things modern instead of the old-world romance the area called for.

It wasn't until I made my way through the other five boxes that I had to count to ten before speaking to her. They were filled with knickknacks. The color scheme was fine, but they would clutter the space and throw off the scale. Not to mention, they were not the correct time period.

"Celia, may I speak with you a moment?" I motioned for her to follow me into the room off reception. Five minutes went by before she graced me with her gazelle-like presence.

"Those extra items were not authorized for purchase.

We've discussed that all changes are to go through me for approval."

Thin ruby-red lips curved into a smirk, and she looked down her artesian straight nose at me. "Stone will appreciate them. They're in the same family as many of the items chosen for his last hotel renovation."

I rubbed the bridge of my nose and counted again. So she'd mimicked what was done before. But why? To get out of doing any additional research or work, or because she thought Stone would appreciate her attention to the details of what he'd chosen for another hotel? With a Herculean effort, I kept my voice at an even tone. "This is your last warning, Celia. You have one more chance to correct this, or you'll be demoted as the lead designer on this project."

"Oh, sweetheart." Celia leaned down, so we were at eye level. "That'll never happen. You can't touch me."

Ah, the uncle on the board and her family's association with Stone's. But this was business, and the company grievances against her were well-documented. "Is that your verbal refusal to return the unauthorized purchases?"

"I don't answer to you. Not now, not ever. When Stone—"

"You do, Celia. Tiffany and Mr. Crenshaw have repeatedly confirmed that." Making a mental note to document Celia's obstinance as soon as I returned to my desk, I went over to Delilah and Betty and tasked them with straightening out the order. One more intentional mistake, and I wouldn't have to deal with Celia as the lead designer. That thought comforted me as I made my way to the lower level.

I exited the narrow stairwell to a dark and dreary basement. The hairs on the back of my neck stood on end, and I glanced over my shoulder, sure I'd see someone lurking behind me. Nobody was there, and I chased away my nerves. Without realizing it, I'd stepped forward, my fingers trailing over the worn and dingy wallpaper as if I'd done this same motion many times before.

The dank, musty smell faded, and in its place, a hint of strong coffee permeated the hallway. As if in a dream, my eyes glazed over, and I took another step, trusting my feet to lead the way as if they had before, while a haze blanketed my mind, warping time. Taking me back—*to him.*

The silk of my dress swirled around my legs, whispering over the tops of my slippers. As I moved closer to the wall, the long fabric of my mauve skirt kissed the empty hallway. Soft flickering light cast shadows on the worn floor, and I shivered from the risk of getting caught, mixed with the compulsion to seek out Cristiano.

A door opened, and the strong aroma of coffee mingled with cedar in an intoxicating blend. A warm flush crept over my cheeks. All I had to do was lift my gaze, and he'd be there. It didn't matter where we were. We always sensed one another when the other was near.

The slight weight of the silver chain at my neck, where the pendant of Saint Valentine rested that he'd given me, was cool against my skin. My satin-covered feet faltered, and with agonizing slowness, I sought him out. I wasn't supposed to be down here. It was scandalous, forbidden. But I couldn't deny our connection, the love that'd blossomed from our first meeting. We were destined for each other. He was the other half of my soul, and we both swore we would find a way to be together, despite my family and society's blind prejudice to his station.

"Francesca."

Smoke and sin. His voice washed over me, and I swayed at the decadence of his verbal caress, longing for the physical one that would soon follow. In delicious increments, my hungry gaze traveled up his strong legs, lingering on where he'd shoved a hand in his pocket, then to his narrow waist, solid chest, and broad shoulders that leaned against the open doorway to his room. But when I got to his devastatingly handsome face, our surroundings faded away, and I was forever lost.

Closing the distance, he enveloped me in his strong embrace. This was home. We'd find a way to be together. We had to. After all, there was no fighting destiny.

Boom. A loud crash reverberated above me likely from the construction crew, jarring me back to reality—to the present. *What was that?* My head pounded and my heart rate had yet to return to normal, thudding against my rib cage as if I'd sprinted.

A gnawing emptiness consumed me as I stood rooted to the scuffed floor in the lifeless hallway, devoid of the gorgeous Cristiano and the promises that had smoldered in his dark eyes. The heat that had spread like wildfire while caught in the vision extinguished, leaving me chilled to the bone.

Not more than three feet away, his door was ajar, and I rushed forward and burst into the room, yearning for another vision of him. Tears misted then grew heavy and clung to my lashes before tumbling down my icy cheeks.

I turned in a slow circle, the windowless room dark, devoid of furniture, and of Cristiano. But in the recess of my mind, a faint hint of coffee beans teased my memories, and I felt him still. With a flick of my finger, I pulled up the flashlight on my iPad and shone it around the tiny space.

The walls were bare, and a thick layer of dust lined the old, narrow, wood plank floor. There weren't any amenities in this room. It was square and lacking comfort. Without looking, I knew I'd passed a small closet by the stairs where brooms and such would have been. A community kitchen with the essentials would be down here and had escaped my notice as I was drawn to this room in particular.

I set the iPad in the corner, angling it, so the light spilled across the room, illuminating much of the floor and walls. A rectangle of wallpaper was less worn where a picture must have hung, and a small crease with a bubble behind it drew me closer. As in the hallway, I trailed my fingers along the wall rounding on the spot that held my focus—until the toe of my shoe caught on an uneven portion of flooring, and I tripped, landing on my knees. Pain shot into my kneecaps, traveling along my legs, and jolting to my stomach. I shifted to rest on my hip and forearms, my body locked in place as nausea held me in its grip. I sucked in air through my nose, frantically swallowing the pooling saliva back down, willing myself not to throw up.

Cold sweat beaded along my hairline and upper lip. Minutes passed, and with each one, the pain and sickness faded. I waited a while longer until the ache dulled enough to shift so I could see what I'd tripped over. One of the floorboards had a notch, big enough to fit two of my fingers under it. That had to be what I'd caught my shoe on. Moving closer, I slipped the tips of my fingers beneath the board and pulled. It loosened, and I was able to remove it from the floor. Instead of a subfloor, there was a small hole.

Needing more light, I got the iPad and shone the flashlight inside. There was something there. A whisper of air teased the loose tendrils of hair at my neck, and I shivered. It felt as if I wasn't the only one hovering expectantly to reveal what was concealed beneath the floor long ago.

I moved for a better angle with caution for my bruising knees. My hand would fit, but I wasn't sure if the object would clear the narrow opening. I yanked on the edge of the floorboard closest to me, but it didn't budge. But the other easily gave, and I quickly removed it. With hands that shook, I retrieved the hidden treasure from its resting place.

With a brush of my hand, I swept the thick layer of dust

from the box. Simple in design, it resembled an old cigar case. I nibbled on my bottom lip, torn. The aroma of coffee swelled, and I swore a hand cupped my shoulder from behind, but when I looked, there was no one there. Even so, here, and in Cristiano's former room, I was comforted. I had to see what he'd left because I knew without a doubt that this belonged to him. The box had to go to Stone. It was his building—and I'd give it to him, but not until after I looked inside.

CHAPTER 10

With the cigar box clutched against my chest, I hurried down the hall from my old room to Stone's suite. All my stuff was packed up to move. My suitcase bumped along behind me, and my bag hung from my shoulder, pressed tightly to my side. It was convenient that he was on the same floor. He wouldn't be back for at least an hour from the board meeting, which left me time to read over Cristiano's letters.

After using the keycard he'd given me, I pushed open the heavy wood door then set my suitcase off to the side. A beautiful sitting room with deep red settees and armchairs were arranged around a dark coffee table. Floor to ceiling drapes framed oversized windows and French doors that led to the balcony.

I dropped my handbag at my feet and sat on the luxurious couch, the cigar box held carefully between my hands. Resting it on my lap, I opened the lid to peer inside. My heart raced as I brushed my fingers over the aged, folded sheets of paper secured by a pale-pink ribbon. Part of me realized I shouldn't touch them with my bare hands, but I couldn't help myself. An odd duality came over me, and it was as if I was close to him once more—home.

In the back of my mind, I recognized the pull Stone had over me, similar to what I'd felt in Francesca toward Cristiano. I mean, I moved into Stone's suite! I couldn't imagine I'd succumb to any other employer suggesting that was the best course of action after a water leak. I would have laughed my head off while checking into another hotel.

I understood what my mother and the psychic were hinting at, directing me toward. Mom had said, "You, my darling daughter, have a different path. Follow it and find your happy." The hotel, learning of Cristiano and Francesca, and finally, Stone. This was my destiny, and I was going to grasp it with both hands.

The emotions from discovering the notes brought images forward from another time, and I let them unfold as if I was immersed in a dream. It was like they were my memories, but at the same time, they weren't. I let myself drift, envisioning how it had all begun. Like the frames of a movie, the present faded and the past materialized.

Cristiano had flashed that pretty necklace while *Madre* wasn't looking. It was how I knew where to find the messages he'd left me: the third stone from the bottom of Juliet's Wall and near the far corner. There were places the mortar was missing, and people secreted love letters in the crevices. But the one where he left notes for me had a lighter vein of color dissecting the brick, and if it weren't for his whispered words as he had passed by me, I wouldn't have known to remove it. Loosened, I was able to pull it out and retrieve the hidden notes during our stay.

Fortunately for me, there was always a crowd in the square by Juliet's Wall, enough so that I could maneuver the stone without *Madre* seeing on our afternoon strolls while she and several women engaged in conversation. Each handwritten note sent a surge of joy, and my heart raced as I fell deeper in love with the handsome boy who I feared my parents would forbid me from entertaining a future with.

I feared our love would end in similar tragedy to the famed Romeo and Juliet. We couldn't let it. My heart thudded with excitement upon learning of all he planned—the moonlit rendezvous away from the prying eyes of my family and the hotel staff and guests. He spoke to my soul with the beautiful words and vows of love, devotion. He was the one I wanted. Somehow, I would convince my parents of this as well.

At the very least, the notes gave me comfort in his intentions. I traced the beautiful script where he'd penned my name. I couldn't let my parents find them, so I had Cristiano keep all our secret messages together. Because should we be found out, they'd whisk me away, and I would never see him again. We'd thought we had the time and a plan.

Time wasn't in our favor then.

I blinked away the distant memories. A sense of familiarity washed over me as I gazed at the same script from the vision scrawled over the letters in the box.

With hands that shook, I tugged the ribbon until the pounding at the door stilled my fingers. That couldn't be Stone. It was at least a half hour too soon.

With infinite care, I placed the antique box on the coffee table and then went to see who was here. I pulled open the heavy doors, my greeting caught in my throat at who stood there—Celia—and instead, I coughed. What the hell could she want?

Wait a minute. My eyes narrowed on her equally stunned expression. Then I took in what she was wearing. Gone was the outfit from earlier, and in its place was a formfitting full-length black evening gown that plunged at the neckline. Diamonds decorated her ears and neck. The ruby-red lipstick was replaced with a deep crimson, and her eyes were carefully lined in black, the shadow matching a smoky nighttime look. In her hands were two champagne flutes and a bottle of Dom Perignon.

I leaned against the doorframe while keeping one hand firmly on the edge of the door so she couldn't force her way inside.

"What are you doing here?" Her shrill voice crackled with outrage.

This wasn't a confrontation I needed tonight, and I crossed my arms over my chest. "I would ask you the same question."

A smirk replaced the shock. "Stone and I have plans this evening."

"No, you don't." This woman was stalkerish crazy. "But if you'd like, I can reach him on his cell and let him know that you're here, after hours, and at the door to his suite."

She crossed her arms over her barely covered chest. "Go right ahead."

"Fine." Stone had better answer. I needed this problem dealt with, and no matter what I told her, I had a strong sense she wouldn't listen. Dialing his number, I tapped the button for the speaker. He answered after the first ring.

"Everything okay?"

Celia's lips parted, and I held up a finger, momentarily throwing her off as I quickly said what I needed to first. "I've got you on speaker. Celia is at our door and claims you have plans with her tonight."

"I don't." The finality in his tone should have been enough for her, but I knew it wouldn't be. She had delusions of grandeur where he was concerned.

But his words were all I needed. She started talking over me, something about a gala event she knew about from her uncle. One she was assured Stone had planned to attend.

What she wasn't privy to was that he'd donated a large sum but had declined the invitation. Something I was well aware of since I had full access to his schedule and handled notifying them myself. "I'll be documenting this unprofessional incident. This is the third strike. You're demoted from lead designer and will report to Delilah. And, Celia, be careful not to make another mistake." Aside from having to raise my voice to be heard above hers, I kept my tone professional.

"This is absurd. Do you have any idea who I am? You're nobody." Celia snarled, her voice rising to greater heights to be heard through the cell. "Stone, she has no right talking to me how she is. Fire this woman."

"That's not going to happen. I've told you multiple times you answer to Adeline, which you've blatantly ignored. What she said stands. You need to leave the building, Celia," Stone said, the exhaustion bleeding through the line.

"Thanks, Stone. I'll handle it from here." With the press of a button, I switched the phone off speaker and held it to my ear. Celia didn't need to hear the rest of our conversation. And after, it was time to put an end to her outlandish behavior. Tomorrow I would put Delilah in charge of leading the team. "I'll see you shortly." After his confirmation as to being ten minutes away, I disconnected the call, realizing we'd have to have the conversation about the letters later. For tonight, I'd stash them away.

"You have no right to be here," she fumed. "Wait until my uncle hears about this."

"I have every right." I held my hand up so she could get a good look at the rock on my finger. Her eyes narrowed with malicious intent, but I pressed on, driving home what I hoped would put a stop to her disillusions. "I live here with Stone."

Fury blazed in Celia's gaze before she stomped away to the elevator. Before she stepped inside, she glanced over her shoulder, her voice snide and a devious smirk shaping the curve of her mouth. "Does he know about Tommy?"

Stone

THE DAY HAD CREPT BY AT A SNAIL'S PACE. I'D LOST COUNT OF the number of times I'd checked my phone to gauge how soon I could put an end to the board meeting. What I wanted was to leave and go to my suite where Adeline would be.

After I had excused myself to take her call and deal with the Celia fiasco, I knew it was time. As quickly as I could, I wrapped up the meeting and left. I should have felt guilt, but I didn't. With a push to the heavy double doors, I entered my suite. The sitting room was empty. Where was she? Setting my briefcase next to the hallway table, I went in search of her, giving in to the sense of urgency I'd been feeling since leaving her side.

There was something inside me that was tied to her, recognized her on another level. I'd worked hard to succeed, to grow my business to a top Fortune 500 company over the past five years. I hadn't ignored my instincts along the way, and I wouldn't when it came to Adeline.

I couldn't stop thinking about her. Damn the consequences. We'd already crossed a line.

Loosening my tie, I headed for her room at the same time she exited it. My hands automatically gripped her arms to stop her from careening into me. She let out a startled laugh, her blue eyes sparkling, and I gave into doing what I'd wanted to from the first time I'd seen her.

I drew her close, keeping her focus locked on me as I

moved with infinite slowness to afford her time to pull away if she wanted. My intentions were clear in my touch as I slid one hand to her hip and the other to cup the back of her neck. Her hands automatically went to my waist, her lips parted in surprise, and I dipped my head to capture her mouth with mine.

On a groan, I devoured her soft, decadent lips. Parting them wider, I explored, tasting her, lost in the sensations I'd only felt with this woman. She melted in my arms, and her moan filled my mouth, stoking my desire to greater heights. I would never get enough of her.

Heat spiraled through me at the way she responded, how she felt. If I wasn't careful, the moment would get away from me, and things would move much faster than I'd intended. When she pressed against my chest with her palms, I drew back, giving her the space she asked for. But I instantly felt the loss as my arms fell away. We stared at one another, our chests rising and falling rapidly.

"What was that?" Her wide eyes conveyed her surprise, but her dilated pupils told me she had been just as affected as I was.

"That was something I've wanted to do since I first held you in my arms."

Adeline toyed with a patron saint pendant around her neck, and when I looked closer, my heart stopped. "Where did you get that?"

She frowned. "I've had this since I was young. My mom bought it for me when I saw it at a consignment shop." A mischievous grin spread across her face. "I had a bit of a meltdown and refused to leave without it. Why?"

"It's something I've seen before." I shoved the conjured memory and similarity of the necklace aside. I ran my fingers through my hair, exhaustion settling over me. Needing her, I laced our fingers. "Are you hungry?"

"No. I know you said we would eat, but it's late. I made you a sandwich. I can grab it, and we can sit on the couch?"

"That sounds good." And a drink. I needed one of those. I went over to the bar and poured two fingers of bourbon. "Want one?" I raised the glass as she entered, plate in hand. At her nod, I fixed one for her too.

Her hair was in a loose braid, and she wore a T-shirt and jeans. It had become a habit to read her graphic tees to gain a deeper insight to her emotions. She had an obsession with them, and I was quickly realizing I did as well. A scan of the words plastered across her enticing chest and I chuckled, my mood instantly lightening. It read: "You had me at I hate that bitch too." With a shake of my head, I traded conspiratorial grins with her because on that we were in a hundred percent agreement.

After placing the plate with my food on the coffee table, she accepted the drink I offered. I took a sip then replaced it with the sandwich. I needed to refuel.

"How did the meeting go?" She tucked her legs underneath her.

I devoured half the sandwich before answering. "It went well, productive. I gave Maxwell, Celia's uncle, a heads-up about how things weren't going well with her employment. He didn't seem surprised."

"I hope that doesn't become a problem should she be let go."

"It won't." Celia was the last thing I wanted to discuss with her. Instead, I wanted to get to know her more. I already knew that I liked to work alongside her. She had a quick mind and great ideas. "Do you miss your friends or hometown?"

The corners of her mouth upturned, and her eyes crinkled. "My friends, yes, my hometown, no. Not even a little. I lived there my entire life. I have a grand plan to travel and a long list of places to go. This amazing job will enable me to take vacations and fulfill that wanderlust like I never could have before."

"Well, you do get four weeks of vacation a year. Plus, there would be opportunities to work alongside me at my other hotels." I had every intention of having her come with me, but now was not the time. We were feeling our way around each other, and I wanted her to be comfortable. Because I had long-term goals where she was concerned. She just didn't know it yet. "Did most of your friends find jobs upon graduating?"

"Yes. My best friend, Eileen, is a travel writer. Which is perfect really." Her eyes sparkled, and a becoming rose dusted her cheeks. "I can visit her wherever she is when I take a vacation, or even a weekend visit." She nibbled on her lip. "What about you? What do you do when you're not working? Do you have hobbies?"

She was cute. "Of course. I don't have a lot of time outside of my company, but I make sure to volunteer in the children's cancer wing in whatever state I'm in each month." I didn't want to talk about this, but it was close to my heart, and the only way for her to let me fully into hers was if I did the same. "I had a younger sister who died at the age of six to lymphoma. Giving back helps to ease a little of the pain and to keep her close. My entire family does as well."

"I'm so sorry. I didn't know." Tears misted her eyes, and she covered my hand with hers. "Cancer is hell."

"It is, and it doesn't discriminate based on age or the goodness of the person, the unreached potential."

We sat in a comfortable silence, and I appreciated Adeline even more for it. My sister was special, and I wanted to share some of her with Adeline.

"She was this little spitfire." I laughed as a memory resurfaced. "She was in this Wonder Woman phase, any female superhero actually, and she'd convinced us to drag all the pillows from the couches into the foyer. We had this grand staircase, and she planned to slide down it and then capture the villain—who happened to be our brother Caden, her twin. He played his role a little too well, probably because of all the crazy stunts Cyn put him through."

"Cyn?"

"Short for Cynthia." I repressed the full-body shudder at the thought of the fear from that day. "She almost did it until she was three-fourths of the way down and one of the missiles, Nerf gun foam bullets, hit her in the face. She lost her grip and fell. By some miracle, she'd landed on a stack of the pillows and was okay." I shook my head. "We weren't. Mom found out and must have yelled at us for a good half hour. It didn't matter. My brothers and I would do anything Cyn wanted. She had that kind of energy, enthusiasm for life."

"She sounds amazing. I wish I could have met her."

Adeline's quiet voice brought me back, and I let go of the past. My cell rang, and I ignored it, caught up in the moment and memories of my sister, until I saw Tiffany's name pop up.

Lifting it from the table, I accepted the FaceTime call. Tiffany's smiling face came into view. "Is everything okay?"

"I had the baby." Her grin stretched impossibly wider, and she held the phone farther away. In her arms was a swaddled baby with a blue knit cap. "We named him Antonio after Aaron's grandfather."

My congratulations blurred with Adeline's squeal of, "He's so cute!"

Tiffany's eyes bulged, and she laughed. "Adeline's there?"

Adeline grabbed my hand, changing the angle of the phone, so it would include her as she scooted close to me. "Yeah, a pipe burst in my room, so I'm staying in the guest room here." She waved it away. "Tell me all the details. What time was Antonio born? How much does he weigh? How are you feeling?"

Tiffany giggled, and I knew she'd read between the lines with our living arrangements. "You and I are going to talk. We'll circle back around to the room situation later." She let out a sigh, and her features softened. "I'll tell you more of the details another time, Adeline, like what the labor was like." She winked at me, and I was glad to be spared those details. "Antonio was born this morning. I feel great now, just tired. He's six pounds, twelve ounces, and nineteen inches long. He's perfect."

Adeline and I chatted with her and Aaron for a few minutes until her eyes drooped from exhaustion. We said our goodbyes, and after disconnecting, I draped an arm around Adeline and leaned back on the couch. I clicked on the television when she yawned, turning to the news. She rested her head on my shoulder, and while the anchor droned on about whatever it was he was saying, my mind puzzled out how to keep her by my side and engaged in a career she found satisfying. Because there was no way I was going to be happy if she managed a hotel while I was halfway around the world.

CHAPTER 11

STONE

Sleep never came easily in this city for me, even when deep in REM, the sheets would tangle around my legs, imprisoning me here, stealing my chance to escape. Tonight was no different, and yet another dream held me in its vice.

"What do you think you're doing, Cristiano?" *Padre's* voice shook with a combination of fear and outrage.

I raked my hair back, torn between my heart and mind. "I can't stop thinking about her. Please understand. If I don't try, then nothing will be gained. I'll live the rest of my life wondering." I rapped my knuckles against the worn wood table where we sat in our small room in the basement of the inn, where the staff's lodgings were. It was dark and cramped, but we made the most of it.

I understood what he was telling me, but my heart did not. Francesca was meant for a man of means, someone worthy of her hand, while my station was beneath that of her family's. Her parents would worry I was after her inheritance. She didn't share those beliefs, and we'd talked of a future together. It wouldn't always be like this, with me working at the inn. I had plans.

But Francesca trumped my wildest dreams, and I couldn't get her off my mind. I hadn't expected to meet her, my soul's other half. With a mere glance, she'd set my world ablaze. We'd even entertained running away together, starting fresh elsewhere beyond the reach of her parents. But I couldn't do that to her, and she shut the idea down out of worry for what her family would do to my *padre*. Even with the obstacles against us, we were determined to find a way to be together.

The undelivered message I'd written before my shift this morning burned a hole in my pocket, as did the necklace I'd purchased for her. It was a pendant with an engraving of Saint Valentine, the patron saint of lovers. I'd gone to our spot, the hiding place behind the loose stone, to leave her another note and found the necklace returned. My heart thundered in my ears, a sense of acute panic riding my heels. She wouldn't have removed it willingly. Not after all we'd said to one another, the connection we shared. We were meant for one another.

The heavy sigh across our worn table told me more than I wanted to hear. It couldn't be true. She couldn't have gone. "Tell me she's here," I demanded. "That she hasn't left."

Indecision deepened the grooves in my *padre's* forehead. "She'll be gone within the hour."

I pushed myself up and away from the table. In three strides, I was at our door, the glass knob tight in my grip as I twisted it with a turn and push. *There's still time.*

Taking the narrow stairs two at a time, I burst from the opening and into the kitchens. The smell of eggs, fresh baked bread, and bacon saturated the air. Ignoring my growling stomach, I skirted around the busy cooks, avoiding the swat from the head chef for dashing through and jostling Isabella, one of the waitstaff, as she brought plates in from the dining hall. Nothing mattered past reaching Francesca's side in time —stopping her.

Maneuvering to the edge of the rooms as I passed through, I wove through early risers as carefully and fast as possible. My long strides took me to the reception area through ornate arches. The high-pitched sound of her *madre's* laughter diminished as they rose from the settee. I increased my pace, uncaring what her parents would think.

Francesca was mine. I would not let her go.

As I neared, my gaze found hers. Tears ran openly down her stunning face, and the despair written across her features almost doubled me over. A slight notch of her head, and then she whispered in her mother's ear. We'd played this game before over the last two weeks.

Pivoting on my heels, I changed directions and pushed open the glass doors to the courtyard, stepping to the side and out of sight. Her mother would have been fed an excuse, and we'd gain a few minutes alone. It didn't take long until she joined me. In a flurry of satin and beads, she was in my embrace, and all was right in my world, at least for a few moments.

The quiver that ran through her confirmed my worst fears, and the meaning behind the abandoned necklace was a dose of reality I didn't want. "Don't go."

A sob burst from her perfect lips. "They saw us together. We leave in a few minutes. Cristiano, I—"

"Shh." I caressed her cheek with my thumb, cupping the side of her face. I hated to see the naked pain in her eyes and would do anything to ease her worry.

"I didn't think I would see you, be able to say goodbye." Her sea-blue eyes swam with tears. "I left you a note…"

I couldn't tell her it would be all right, because I didn't know. I wanted her to remain with me to start a new life. But was that fair to her? At this point, I wouldn't be able to provide for her as her family could.

Our situation was crushing me; my head was underwater with the reality of what was about to happen. "Somehow, someway, we *will* be together."

"Promise?" Her wide blue eyes begged for reassurance.

"Yes, I would risk everything to find you again." I bent my head and took her lips with mine. My blood heated, rushing through my veins, at the touch of my tongue to her hers. She parted for me, and I teased her mouth open farther, exploring the softness within. Our heartbeats aligned, and I swear my soul sang to hers. There wasn't much time, and with her in my arms, I knew I would lose track of it too fast.

With reluctance, I released her swollen lips as the sound of raised voices pierced our sanctuary. Her parents had found us. "I love you, Francesca, and vow that I will find you again."

The smell of coffee pulled me from my dreams, and I woke disoriented. The beans were different, not quite as intoxicating as I remembered in the small room Cristiano had shared with his *padre*. I had to work to make sense of my surroundings. Gone was the small, depressing room with the two narrow cots and worn wooden table. Instead, I lay on a king-sized mattress with light streaming across it from the large windows.

My heart hurt as Francesca slipped away from me again. But it was just a dream. Something conjured from my imagination, yet it was innately powerful and had left me shaken. Just like then, I knew I couldn't lose her, would do anything to find her again.

The two worlds—both imagined and real—collided, and I swore I could see the make-believe woman looking over her shoulder as she exited through the doorway. Long honey-blond hair fell in loose waves down her back, obscuring the narrow waist that moments ago I'd spanned with my hands. Her voice whispered to me, carried on the fading moonbeams, luring me to her. Where she went, I'd follow. Always.

The sense of inadequacy from when I was with her, the frustration over not being able to fight for her, roared to the surface. I wasn't that guy. I'd amassed an empire. On the heels of that thought came Adeline, my fake fiancée, and how quickly she'd come to matter to me. Urgency fueled me to do something, to change our relationship even further.

Sitting up, I ran my palms over my face, chasing away the remnants of the dream. What the hell was wrong with me? Glass clinked in the other room, and I shoved the covers back. Without making a sound, I passed through the open door from my room and made my way to the kitchenette.

Adeline faced away from me, pouring a cup of coffee and wearing black yoga pants and a white T-shirt. Her hair fell down her back in silvery waves, not the gold ones from my dream. Even so, it didn't matter. My subconscious recognized her.

In slow motion, she turned, and with each increment, her features were revealed. I knew her. It wasn't that I'd seen her before because she worked for me. The curve of her jaw, the wide, almond-shaped blue eyes, and that perfectly formed mouth. The girl from my dreams superimposed over Adeline's image, and I had to blink several times. Their similarities were uncanny.

"Coffee?" Adeline broke through my thoughts.

"Yes." *Goddamn.* What was wrong with me? My hands curled around the edge of the granite countertop as she poured me a cup. We'd kissed last night, and it would have gone further, but she drew back, and I had to respect her wish not to move too fast. The tight grip on the stone kept me from reaching out to her. As she moved around the island, what I wanted, no needed, became clear—her. And this time, I wasn't going to let her go.

Minutes ticked by, and she left to get dressed for the day. When she was ready, she exited her room and then rushed around the small kitchen area, putting her dishes away. As she slipped on her heels, a reminder chime sounded from her cell phone. She glanced down at the screen, and my mind continued to whirl with possibilities. I wanted something different, real, with her.

"Hey, you have a conference call at eight."

"Right." I pushed away from the peninsula, downed the last sips of my coffee, and then went to get ready. Refocused, I broke free from the clinging fog of my dream. In record time, I'd showered and dressed. I straightened my tie when the door slammed shut behind Adeline as she left for the office I had set up in the other suite.

I made a mental note to check in with Tiffany in a few days to see how she and the baby were doing. Eventually, she wanted to come back to work but at a part-time capacity. I promised her I'd figure out how to make that happen. Plus, she wanted to stay in Verona due to her husband's job. Now that I had Adeline working with me, it was an ideal situation.

On the way out, I grabbed my laptop with a few seconds to spare. I was cutting it close, which was unusual for me. Once in the office I shared with Adeline, I gave her a brief nod as I dialed into the call and then deposited my laptop on my desk.

Five minutes into listening to problems and resolutions about our new internet carrier and scheduling platform for the Verona hotel, Adeline rapped against the doorframe. I motioned her closer.

"Vince Mariucci is on the line for you." She kept her voice low. "Do you want to take it or schedule a time to talk with him?"

"No. I'll take it." She went back to her desk while I extracted myself from the meeting with plans to check in on the progress they'd made in a few hours. The light flashed on the landline. Switching to that phone, I exchanged greetings with Vince.

"I've decided to award Stone Enterprises the bid for the purchase of the Bianca."

"That's fantastic news, Vince."

"Would you and Adeline be able to meet Margaret and me for dinner to discuss the details?"

A huge sense of relief filled me. I was almost free of staying in Verona, the place that, for some reason, kept dragging me down. "We'd be happy to go over the contract at dinner."

We set a time and place, which meant Adeline and I would have to leave here mid-to-late afternoon. Rather than updating her about the need to reschedule the rest of my day, I went in search of her to tell her in person.

"So?" A wide smile stretched her lips. "Did you get it?"

"We did." In two strides, I was around her desk and pulling her to her feet. My arms wrapped her in a tight hug. Joy filled her laugh, and my mood lifted to impossible heights.

"We did it!" Winning the bid wasn't the only thing that had elevated my outlook so drastically. "We leave this afternoon." With reluctance, I released her.

"Oh, that's great." She ran a hand down her pale-pink blouse, smoothing out any wrinkles I'd made.

"If you can rearrange my schedule to accommodate that as well as freeing tomorrow morning, we'll have dinner with the Mariuccis and stay the night, coming back in the early afternoon."

"Dinner in Venice. Sure. You'll get no argument from me." She swiped a finger across her iPad to wake it up as I took a step toward my office and the mounds of work that waited for me. "Oh, maybe we can talk tonight? I wanted to tell you something last night, but with Celia crashing your place and having to demote her…"

"Yes. We'll talk." I left her with that, turning so she wouldn't see the devious glint that no doubt shone in my eyes. Things were about to get complicated.

CHAPTER 12

ADELINE

With each visit to Venice, I fell deeper in love with the floating city. Here, with Stone, all his stressors from Verona faded, and he was charming and attentive, so much that I could picture the contract that bound us together as unnecessary, that we would have chosen this path organically.

I sipped my wine as we chatted amicably with Vince and Margaret at a canal-side restaurant that was less fancy than the one we'd previously gone to. The train ride and water taxi here flew by as Stone and I had immersed ourselves in work so that we could enjoy a weekend in Venice. I couldn't believe it when he suggested we stay and had enthusiastically agreed.

We dropped our bags at the hotel and then made the decision to sign the contract after dinner in Vince's office. Stone and I were both more than ready to enjoy the evening. Not only that, but away from the Verona property, this could be a better place to talk to him about what I'd found in Cristiano's room. And I would when we got back to our room tonight.

Vince and Stone went over the contract while Margaret and I half-listened. We chatted about where she and her husband planned to travel next month. I was excited for her. "Santorini. I can only imagine how beautiful that must be."

Margaret sighed. "That's where we went on our honeymoon, and this will be the first time we've been back since."

The island boasted white-washed homes and stunning views of either the ocean or lagoon. "Will you stay on the side with the Aegean Sea or the lagoon?" I rested my elbows on the table, leaning forward. The prospect of the history and myth of the Greek island made it one of the top contenders on my travel wish list. "It's rumored that Atlantis sunk into the Aegean Sea. I would think that area, well either side really, would be magical."

"It is. For our honeymoon, we stayed seaside, but this time around, we thought we'd try the lagoon. It's an experience not to be missed. You and Stone must go sometime."

A small smile curved my lips, and I stole a glance at Stone as he turned to me, a matching expression on his chiseled face.

"We'll make a point to visit there after Verona is complete, and we have the necessary infrastructure in place in Venice. If that's top on your travel list, Adeline, then we'll go."

If only this was real. Even so, I couldn't stop the yearning from encasing my words. "Yes, I'd love to visit Greece."

He chuckled. "We can get you a couple of new T-shirts to add to your collection when we're there."

My heart warmed at his teasing smile—he got my silly addiction to graphic tees.

He winked at me before facing our dinner companions. "Adeline has a collection of shirts with different sayings. Sometimes, she expresses her feelings through them if I'm too dense to read between the lines. My favorite one of late is: I'm fine. But there's a massive blood splatter underneath the caption. It's a close tie to yesterdays: I'm not in a bad mood. Everyone is just annoying."

"Don't scare them away!" I shared a look with Margaret, who was wiping away a tear from laughter. "Remember," I sing-songed, "I've got secrets on you too."

"Addy." I knew that gruff voice behind me. *Tommy?* A jolt of panic shot through me. *My ex from college?* I jumped to my feet. My knee banged on the table, rattling the dishes, as I spun around. He loomed over me, scowling. Shit, this wouldn't be good.

"What are you doing here?" Not my finest moment. Stone came to his feet, his hand settling on the small of my back, and I glanced at him over my shoulder.

"So this is the guy?" Tommy's gaze dropped to the rock on my finger. "You're engaged to me, not him."

"We weren't." I shook my head, flashing an apologetic smile to Vince and Margaret. "I need a minute." Stone's dark eyes narrowed on him like a heat-seeking missile. I had to defuse this situation.

I frantically searched for a quiet corner where we could talk. A small alcove at the corner of the restaurant would have to do. "Good to see you, Tommy." I quickly introduced him as a friend from school to Stone and the Mariuccis before I grasped his mammoth arm and tugged for him to come with me. He did. I was under no illusion that I was able to make him go physically. I was just glad he didn't create a scene back there.

We wove through the outdoor tables until we were at the outer edge of the restaurant near a row of empty gondolas tied to the pier. I had to get rid of him. I should never have left without having another discussion with him. But seriously, how many times did he need to hear we're through?

"What are you doing here, Tommy?" I crossed my arms

over my chest and worked hard to keep my expression neutral. He curved his hulking form toward me, so his face was closer to mine.

Anger flashed in his dark-brown eyes, and his fists clenched at his sides. "I came to find you. This is my last year, and the NFL Combine is this February. You know what that means, right?"

Crap. I felt for him, I did. But we didn't work together as a couple. "I do, and you're going to get scouted by a fantastic team. I know it. Your skills are on point, and you're one of the best defenders around. You've got nothing to worry about, and I'm looking forward to watching you play in the NFL after you graduate."

His jaw hardened with determination. "I love you and need you by my side."

"No, Tommy. You don't." I gave his wrist a squeeze then dropped my hand down by my side. "There is no us. We've been over this so many times. It was interesting running into you here but I've got to go." I wanted to know why he was here, but if we kept talking, I knew precisely how Tommy would react. I needed to wrap up our dinner meeting and get back to the hotel, where Tommy wasn't.

CHAPTER 13

ADELINE

Tommy wouldn't leave, so we decided to take our discussion elsewhere. The walk back, ten-minute water taxi, and subsequent elevator ride to our suite had left me shaken. The five of us were too close, the secrets too tangible.

When we arrived at our floor, Vince and Margaret turned to go in the opposite direction, saying they wanted to check on friends. I took in the confusion in their expressions and mentally cursed myself for blocking Tommy's number.

I had to try to salvage what had happened before they left. "Margaret." She turned, and I stepped close. "I'm mortified you both were pulled into my drama. Tommy and I grew up together, and he's confused about how things ended between us."

"Don't worry about a thing," Margaret said. "I'm sure you'll get everything straightened out."

Anxiety about what would happen to Stone's deal churned in my stomach. "I hope this doesn't have any reflection about how Stone or I would do business. This was…" There were no words.

"Nonsense." Margaret flashed a small smile.

"We're not making any rash judgments," Vince answered. "We'll continue our meeting when everything has calmed down."

After a shaky smile, we parted ways, and I went with Stone to our hotel suite, Tommy following close behind. When the three of us were inside and with the door closed, I turned to face Tommy while Stone stood at my side. His larger-than-life presence was a comfort, but this was my problem to correct. One that I hoped wouldn't shatter his business deal with Vince.

"Why don't we sit down?" I had to try to fix this.

Stone's face was granite, giving nothing away of his thoughts. His arm went around the back of the couch we sat on, and his hand rested on my shoulder. "What the hell is going on?"

Tommy sat on a chair across from us. I dove into my part to try to diffuse the tension radiating off Stone. "Tommy and I weren't engaged. We dated, but I broke it off."

"We're still engaged, Addy," Tommy said through gritted teeth.

Stone's fingers tightened, and he pulled me closer to his side, but I spoke before he could. "No, Tommy, we aren't. It wasn't real, and I gave back your ring." I held up my hand to stop his protest, pleading with my eyes for him to give me a few seconds. "I need to explain to Stone."

I didn't even know how to fix his misguided superstition. The beard tradition was typical. But the one time I wasn't in the stands and they lost a game during playoffs, he viewed my lack of presence as the factor. After that incident in his freshman year, it was mandatory that I was present for all home games. I liked watching him play, but I should have worked to set him straight that my being there didn't affect his playing one bit.

We were both stubborn and argued like siblings. It was a small miracle Tommy had agreed to come back here, to sit quietly, even though he stared at Stone like he was on the line, ready to decimate his opponents on the football field.

Things between Stone and me… I didn't want to jeopardize our relationship, or what could be. I had to share why I put up with some of Tommy's quirks, and why I hadn't resolved things well enough before leaving the States. I met Stone's gaze to explain my connection to Tommy, then I would move into where things got muddy. "Tommy was my neighbor while I lived with my parents." I let myself smile at Tommy because even though things had gone to shit, they weren't always like that.

"We grew up together, climbing trees and racing around the neighborhood. We share history. When he got into football, I would spend hours throwing the ball with him or creating obstacles we could run through to improve his speed and agility. And I liked them too. When Mom died, Tommy was there for me." My eyes misted, and I swallowed hard, fighting the emotion.

"Even when we'd grown apart, he would make me come outside and toss a ball around with him to help get my mind off things. I'll always be grateful for our friendship." I turned to Tommy, swiping a tear from the corner of my eye. "For what you did for me."

"Nothing's changed, Addy." His large hand enveloped mine across the coffee table in a gentle grip as he pulled me forward a little, creating space between Stone and me.

He thought he had me there, but he didn't. We weren't right for each other. Stone appeared relaxed by my side, but his thigh that was pressed against mine was solid and told me another story. I had to keep a lid on the testosterone-inducing words. "We didn't date until college. But it became clear we were better as friends, and I ended the relationship."

I held up my hand once more to stop Tommy from denying it.

"You know I did. It wasn't until my dad got sick that I leaned on you again." My voice cracked, but I pushed myself to give him closure. "It wasn't fair to you. I thought you understood that I didn't want to get back together, that I just needed a friend who knew my family too."

The tears were unstoppable as they rolled down my cheeks. Stone clasped one of my hands in his and squeezed. I wanted to press into him, but with Tommy here, that wasn't a good idea. Not yet.

"I cared about them too." Tommy's fists were clenched and resting on the top of his tree-trunk thighs. "Your dad wanted us to be together. I made that happen, Addy."

"He did say that, but it was because he was scared to leave me all alone when he passed." How was I supposed to make him understand we weren't going to be together without tearing his heart out?

"I fixed everything. I proposed right there, even put the ring on your finger."

"I never said yes, Tommy." I had to work hard to keep my voice calm.

"You didn't say no."

"I did too!" Shit. I took a deep breath and reset. "I told you I didn't want to get married, that we were better as friends."

"Then why didn't you tell your dad? You wore my ring. That meant something."

"It meant—"

"—That's enough," Stone interjected, his gaze burning into Tommy's. He stood, blocking the view between Tommy and me. "You and I need to have a conversation."

"I guess we do," Tommy snapped as he stood to follow Stone. As they made their way past the kitchen, Tommy did what he did best, he poked the bear. "Then I'll be leaving with my fiancée."

"You won't, and she's my fiancée," Stone growled.

I remained on the couch while they headed to the door. The sound of the latch clicked into place after they stepped into the hallway and the door shut behind them. Their voices faded, and I figured they had moved farther down the corridor, possibly near the elevator. A few seconds later, I lost it. God, I missed Mom so much.

I had to pull myself together, and with effort, I did. With a wad of Kleenex, I cleaned up my face as much as I could. Seeing Tommy and having him bring up the stupid engagement stunt he'd pulled brought back too many memories. This situation was… intense.

It was time to gather myself and put an end to this mess. When this was over, I really wanted to put on a T-shirt, yoga pants, and binge-watch some Netflix on the couch with Stone. I needed some downtime.

This wasn't his problem. I needed to deal with Tommy. I dragged myself off the couch to face them. With a turn of the doorknob, I left behind the beautiful room with hand-painted ceiling frescos by artists in the eighteen hundreds and entered the softly lit hallway. I could hear the guys' voices near the elevator, but Vince and Margaret rounded the corner at the same time as I stepped outside our suite, and my step waivered. Stone and Tommy were near the elevator, and their conversation looked heated.

"How are you, dear?" Margaret made the decision for me, and I shifted my direction to them instead of the guys.

I blew out a breath. There were things I wanted to share. They were good people, and after so many years, it was obvious how in love they were. They watched me now with concern, not condemnation. But I understood that while they may like me on a personal level, the scene with Tommy and our fake engagement could impact the business one. I gathered myself to tell them what was going on between Stone and me. "I need to tell you something, and I hope you'll allow me the opportunity to do so."

"Of course," Margaret said. Vince stood at her side, his arm wrapped around his wife's waist.

"Tommy and I are friends. That's all. The engagement between us was something he did for my dad's benefit before he passed away six months ago. He doesn't feel what he should for me, not the way you should for the person you want to marry, to spend the rest of your life with. He's wrapped up in football, and worries about not doing well or getting drafted into the NFL. Stone and I—"

"Are different." Margaret winked, a knowing smile curving her lips.

"Yes." I wanted to share parts of our story. Maybe that would help them see that this drama was a bump along the way but Stone wasn't involved with a crazy person. "The first time I met Stone, we literally slammed into each other. At the time, I probably had jet lag, and he was preoccupied. But when we collided, it was the oddest thing, and to this day, I wonder if I hit my head." I told them of the flashback, of losing consciousness for a few seconds and seeing what seemed like another time in history, one where I was Francesca, and he was Cristiano. About how we'd grown closer while working together. Then the dreams Stone and I had, his dislike for the Verona hotel, and about finding the letters.

Margaret had Vince's hand clasped tightly in hers. "That is one of the most romantic stories I've heard. Venice has our fair share too."

A small smile curved my lips, and I let my worry about them go because she was right, it was romantic, and it was ours.

"Adeline," Stone interrupted, anger radiating from his tense posture.

Shoot, did I do the right thing? Judging from his expression, I wasn't sure. "Did Tommy leave?"

"He will be."

I moved around him and spotted Tommy by the elevator. "I'll go say goodbye then."

"I don't think that's a good idea."

I patted his bicep. "I'll be fine."

Stone

GODDAMN. I RAN MY HANDS THROUGH MY DISHEVELED HAIR. After clearing my throat, I thought about what I wanted to say to them, unsure of what Adeline had told them. Vince's expression gave nothing away. "I owe you both an apology."

"That's not necessary." Vince waved away my words. "Adeline already explained everything."

They were good people, and lying to them didn't sit right with me anymore, but they didn't need to know about our fake engagement too. "This won't change things between the two of us. The mix-up with Tommy will get sorted." I strained to hear Adeline's voice, making sure they were there.

I couldn't stop glancing over my shoulder at the large frame of Tommy's oversized body. Why was he still here? I didn't like Adeline with him. Alone.

"The dreams—" Margaret said.

"—all true," I interrupted. The hairs on the back of my neck rose, and I couldn't shake the feeling that Adeline was in danger. The anxiety, the sheer panic from my last dream, the one I wanted to tell her about, slammed into me with the brutality of an avalanche.

In the vision, my *padre* had told me Francesca was leaving within the hour with her family. I'd never see her again. Why this was happening to us, tore my heart from my chest. I'd raced up the back stairs of the hotel.

When I'd found her, we had only a handful of stolen moments before she was ripped from my life forever.

That wasn't our fate. *This is*. This time, I wouldn't let her go.

Vince was saying something about the contract when the silence registered. Whirling around, I took a few steps down the hallway until the closed elevator door was in sight. She was gone.

"Where are you going?" Vince's asked.

The thud of my feet matched the pounding of my heart as I raced to where they had been. A glance at the elevator showed the numbers going down. The stairs would be the best way to stop Tommy and to help Adeline. They couldn't have gone far. My fingers curled around the door handle, and I yanked it open. Vince appeared in my peripheral vision. I didn't have time for him. "I have to find Adeline; she's all that matters."

CHAPTER 14

"Put me down now!" An explosive combination of anger and mortification churned in my blood. Tommy's arms pinned mine against my side, our chests flush, and my feet dangled from the ground as he carried me out of the elevator.

"No. Not until you see reason." His face scrunched, and a flash of hurt brightened his dark eyes. "How could you leave for Italy like that? You didn't even come talk to me. You ghosted me."

"Are you kidding?" He was exasperating. I loved him, but more like an idiot brother, not in the way he envisioned us. And this... he'd gone too far this time. "I broke up with you. Several times, I made it clear we are only friends. The stunt you pulled by Dad's bedside was sneaky, and you know it."

"You know the pressure I'm under. This is my future. I need you there with me, watching from the stands. What's that gonna look like to the scouts, agents, teams, when my fiancée is in another country, wearing another man's ring?"

"You and I were fake engaged, and it was you who put us in that position." There was no reasoning with him. He thought of me like a good luck charm to be by his side while he waited to find out if he got drafted. Once he was on a team and playing in the NFL, I doubted he would need me. That is, when he figured out his talent didn't depend on rituals and superstitions.

When he got this muleheaded, he wouldn't listen, and we were closing in on the hotel's exit. I wasn't going to leave. The sound of a door banged against a wall somewhere behind us. I hoped it was Stone, but regardless, I needed to do something to get free.

Like when we were kids and he pulled a stunt like this, I leaned my head back, and then whipped it forward. My forehead slammed into Tommy's nose. Pain exploded, radiating to my eyes. The room spun. His yell snapped me out of it. People were running. The sound of their shoes hitting the tile matched the throbbing in my head. Shouts pierced my skull. Tommy's arms loosened, and I wiggled free. As soon as my feet found purchase, I backed away.

Strong arms lifted me. A familiar sizzle at his touch calmed the fight that coursed through me, and I let Stone place me behind his back.

My forehead throbbed. I'd forgotten how much it hurt to head-butt someone. My fingers tangled in Stone's shirt, and I took a few measured breaths while angry male voices filtered in.

"We'll be pressing charges," Stone growled. He took a step toward Tommy.

I melted more for his defense of me, even if it was unwarranted. Tommy would never hurt me. He was a bit much at times and reacted before thinking, but harmless. This was such a mess. I had to straighten it out. Tommy would see reason, eventually.

I stepped around Stone, so I was at his side, crossed my arms over my chest, and glared at Tommy. Stone's hand gripped my hip, anchoring me to him. Several security guards had circled Tommy. A crowd had formed. I wanted to roll my eyes at the scene, but that would've hurt, so I amped up my glare instead. "*What* were you thinking?"

"I need you, Addy." His hand dropped from his nose. My blow to it had caused a small cut on the bridge where blood bloomed. It was broken, no doubt about it. I'd heard the snap when I'd made impact.

"Stop being a knuckle dragger. You don't need me, Tommy." I sighed, needing to get through to him. "You're a gifted athlete. I know you'll get snapped up by the team of your dreams. I don't have anything to do with your skill, and we're friends. That's all. But if you don't get it through your thick skull that that's the only thing we'll ever be, then we're going to have problems, and that won't look good to any potential NFL affiliates if they get wind of this little scenario."

"He won't be playing at all after what he did to you." Anger radiated from Stone, and his grip tightened.

I had to get control of the situation. If Stone heard where Tommy's misguided ideas originated, maybe he'd see reason too. And my guess was that this was due to Celia spying on my incoming texts. Somehow, she had tracked him down. "What did Celia say to you, Tommy?"

Beside me, Stone stiffened and inhaled sharply through his nose. I knew this was the final straw for him.

"That chick called me out of nowhere and told me that this guy was taking advantage of you. I couldn't let anything happen to you, Addy."

Stone felt like granite. "Celia?"

I kept focused on Tommy. Stone would figure everything out. "She lied." My tone softened because this wasn't entirely his fault, and I was feeling guilty about messing up his nose. "While I appreciate you thinking you had to come to my rescue, you should have called, not tried to kidnap me."

His brows scrunched together, and his fists clenched and unclenched at his side. "She sent me a ticket and said I had to hurry. I didn't know what was going to happen, but I owed you. Besides, you blocked me, remember?"

Heat infused my cheeks. "Right. Sorry about that." Something else was going on. "Why do you think you owe me?"

"You did so much for me—all the tutoring. Without you, I wouldn't have passed any of the math classes or done so well on the rest. If my grades had dropped, I could have lost my scholarship. And I didn't want to lose you."

"We're friends. Of course, I would help you. I'll still do that if you need anything. But this"—I motioned between us —"is never going to happen. We're better as friends. Deep down, you know that too. You'll find the person who's right for you. The one who's your personal cheerleader. I know it. And, Tommy, Celia's a snake. Don't ever listen to her or anyone like her again. Talk to me. Think before you act."

A red stain spread across his wide face, and he hung his head. "I've never been very good at that."

I laughed because it was so very true. Jumping off the roof, cliff diving, and racing down the insane road we called the widowmaker on our bikes, careening through intersections without thought. Yeah, we'd both done that, but he was always the instigator. I'd gone along because it pushed me even further out of my comfort zone. In a way, he'd been good for me. Not necessarily some of the dangerous parts, but the rest had been.

The murmurs around us filtered in, and I realized we needed to take this little scene elsewhere.

Tommy held out his hand to Stone with a sheepish half grin. "Sorry, man, but it was Addy. I couldn't let anything happen to my girl."

"She's not your girl," Stone growled. "She's mine."

"Well, maybe not in that sense, I guess." Tommy dropped his hand when it became clear Stone wasn't having anything to do with shaking his. Then his game face replaced the contrite one. "If you ever hurt her, I'll be back."

For that, I grinned. He was sweet, and I would always care about him, just not in any romantic capacity. There was no doubt in my mind he would find someone perfect.

I clapped my hands together, getting everyone's attention. "So, we're good now?"

It took another fifteen minutes until everyone was calm and secure that nothing else would happen. Vince and Margaret dismissed the guards they'd called before stepping into the elevator to try to help, promising we'd talk in the morning. The three of us had sat at a table outside overlooking the water, talking. It was good to clear the air and get our friendship back to where it was meant to be. Not only that, but I had to make sure Stone wouldn't follow through with his threat to mess with Tommy's career. Another half hour and we'd wrapped up our chat. Then Stone and I had made sure Tommy was on a water taxi back to catch the next flight home.

I leaned against Stone. He hadn't stopped touching me the entire time, with his hand in mine or securely around my waist. There was a fierce determination that radiated from him. We stood on the shoreline in front of the hotel, as Tommy's boat grew smaller in the distance.

Waves from the Adriatic Sea broke against the sand, not far from our feet. Inky darkness blanketed the horizon, broken only by the moonlight, and the soft glow of the hotel's outdoor lamps fell short of where we stood. A warm breeze blew off the water, carrying with it tiny drops of sea spray.

"I thought I'd lost you." Stone's somber voice broke the peaceful silence. "Again."

"What do you mean?" I lifted my head from where it rested against him, peering into his eyes. The wind ruffled his hair, and I brushed the fallen strands from his forehead.

"When he was in our room, I had this awful feeling." His voice sounded haunted, pain clinging to the quietly spoken words. "It was like losing you all over again. I know that doesn't make sense, but—"

"—No, it does." I cupped the side of his jaw then slid my hand around to the back of his neck, toying with the thick hair at his nape.

A faint smile curved his mouth, and he closed some of the distance between us, dipping his head toward mine. A shiver of anticipation raced through me, and my knees threatened to buckle. I wanted to taste his lips and feel his arms around me.

"If he'd left with you... I can't fully explain it, but it's as if I've lived through that before, and I couldn't let it happen. Not again."

Waves lapped, filling the silence, and I shook my head, gaze locked on his possessive one. *Never again.* He pulled me closer. Pressed against him, I was incapable of uttering a word. His lips grazed over mine, and my eyelids closed. From the first moment we'd collided in front of the Verona hotel, I'd longed to feel his touch again.

It would never be enough.

He deepened the kiss, exploring, taking his time. My head spun. Desire raged through my body. I wanted him. When he broke the kiss, I sucked in a breath. While he kissed me, I hadn't needed oxygen, just him.

"Come with me." He tucked a long strand of hair behind my ear, his fingers trailing down my cheek and resting on the pulse that fluttered at the base. "Let's go back to our room."

When his hand slipped around my waist and he urged me forward, it took a few seconds until I came to my senses enough to hear the waves breaking against the shoreline. In a daze, I let him lead me from the moonlit beach, through the hotel, and finally to our suite.

The doors clicked shut behind us. I wet my lips. He followed the motion, his eyes hungry. We each took a half step forward, as if an invisible thread was strung taut between us. In a lightning-fast move, he drew me close, and his mouth devoured mine. I lost myself in his touch until he rested our foreheads together, our breaths mingling in hurried pants.

"You drive me crazy." He trailed the pad of his thumb over my lower lip. "Every time you're near, my body reacts, and I can't stop thinking about you. I don't want the separation between us if you manage one of my hotels—"

"But—" I tried to pull back, but he held me fast.

"Shh." His gaze restlessly bounced over my face. "The best part of my day is when you're in it."

All resistance fled, and once more, I melted against him.

"If you go to one of my other hotels, I won't get to see you, interact, just be with you day in and day out. I want this. Us. Work *with* me, because I want to date you, Adeline, and make this fake thing real."

My heart rate sped up, and I let myself trust in us. It wasn't about my career any longer. I'd have that regardless, working side by side with Stone. It was about being happy with the one person I was meant to be with. Finally, I understood what my mom tried to tell me about how she never regretted giving up modeling to be with my dad, to start a family. While a family wasn't my goal, at least not anytime soon, working alongside this man and exploring what was between us was. "I want that too."

"This changes things," he growled. "We're not going back to a platonic work relationship. To hell with the contract."

With a half nod, I dropped all my shields. I didn't want to fight this attraction anymore. "I want you." Nothing past that mattered. I took a step back, and his arms slid away. With unhurried movements, I loosened my hair, so the weighty length fell around my shoulders and down my back. He reached out and fingered a strand then trailed his hand down my arm to grasp my hand in his.

The intricate wall paintings, fresco ceiling, and richly elegant furniture faded as Stone led me into our bedroom. Between his words and actions, everything was changing for the better. Our hands pulled apart as I turned to face him. He slid his arms out of his suit coat then draped it over the arm of the love seat. With his focus locked on me, he worked his tie free then the buttons of his shirt. Discarded, both joined the jacket as I stepped out of my wedges.

Broad shoulders flexed as he moved, and my pulse fluttered at the base of my neck. *So sexy.* Illuminated by moonlight, his taut skin tempted, and my fingers twitched with the need to explore the well-defined contours.

He advanced, and I retreated, as dark promise swam in his eyes. The swoosh of silk from my dress stilled as we paused at the side of our king-sized bed, the champagne duvet pressing against the back of my thighs. Heat radiated off Stone as he crowded me, and I wound my arms around his waist, urging him closer. The touch of his hand at the hem of my dress hitched my breath. With excruciating slowness, his hand moved up the outer side of my thigh, the fabric bunching above his caress.

Beneath my fingers, the muscles in his back shifted and bulged as he lifted his other hand to cup the back of my neck, angling my head for his kiss. I melted against him as his lips brushed back and forth against mine.

Electricity sizzled through my body with his every caress. Soon, I would be a pile of smoking embers. Leashed strength rippled beneath my fingertips as he deepened the kiss, his tongue teasing then insistent.

I quivered with need. His mouth left my lips to trail kisses along my neck. My dress gathered at the tops of my thighs. Putty in his hands, I turned when he guided me. Lifting to my toes, his hips pressed against the curve of my ass, and I arched into him. The bite of his teeth where my neck met my shoulder sent a dizzying wave of desire, and I gasped.

I'd never felt like this with anyone before, and I would have swayed from the overwhelming sensations, but Stone's hand shifted from my neck to my waist, holding me up. With his other hand, he worked my panties free, guiding them down my legs. My body hummed, hypersensitive to his every touch. "Hurry." I couldn't wait much longer. The buildup of desire I fought daily with his nearness boiled to the surface. His gentle caresses changed to urgent, in sync with my escalating need. I didn't want to go slow. I wanted fast and furious.

"I want you now, Adeline." He tugged the hair at my nape, tilting my head, so I met his burning gaze that held such promise over my shoulder. My knees went weak. "Later, I'll explore every inch of you."

I moaned at the image of this larger-than-life man doing things to me that I'd only fantasized about. "Yes."

His forehead rested against my shoulder. I heard the slide of his zipper and then the crinkle of a wrapper. He controlled my body, and as he lifted his predatory gaze, my core exploded with heat, slicking the way for his entry.

My legs shook with anticipation. He pressed against my curves, and I pushed back, needing him to fill me. When his fingers traced my seam, I cried out, arching higher to meet him. A sense of urgency chased the feverish nerve pulses, and when he plunged inside, stretching me, I exploded around him in quivering convulsions.

One hand gripped the duvet and the other on his arm that acted like a steel band around my waist. "Adeline, you're so beautiful." The tug on my hair barely registered as he angled my head to accept his sizzling kiss.

My head swam as sensation after sensation crested in waves, following each powerful thrust. His corded muscles flexed and bulged against my back and beneath my fingertips. When he slid a hand down my stomach to dip between my folds, teasing the sensitive bundle of nerves, I cried out, my body again convulsing around his.

He moved from devouring my lips to my neck. He whispered my name, heightening the aftershocks of my orgasm. Then his moan vibrated against my skin, and as he chased my climax, following with his own.

In his embrace, I clung to him for strength, unsure if my legs would ever work again. A few seconds passed where neither of us was willing to move, the only sound our panting breaths slowly evening out. When he pulled out, I felt empty, wanting him all over again.

No words were necessary as he turned me around then helped me take off my dress. He drew the duvet back then lifted me into the bed. After tying off and throwing away the condom, he stripped out of the rest of his clothes shoved hastily down his thighs and then climbed in bed beside me.

In the glow of the moonlight from the still open windows, something clicked inside of me, aligning everything I could ever want in this one moment. This was what I wanted. And I knew, with Stone by my side, life would never be dull.

His mussed dark hair begged my fingers to run through

it, and his charcoal eyes burned with intense emotion that must have mirrored in my lighter ones. He tugged my body against his. Enveloped in his embrace, I relaxed, tangling my legs with his. Content, we dozed.

I woke sometime in the middle of the night to his fingers tracing the shell of my ear as he tucked my messy hair behind it. A moan parted my lips. I was ready for round two, and with his unhurried touch, I knew he planned to deliver on the promise he'd made earlier. I stretched languidly before his body settled over mine, and I welcomed his weight.

CHAPTER 15

STONE

Vince and Margaret were called away in the middle of the night when their daughter went into labor. Therefore, Adeline and I had left for Verona after breakfast. I scheduled a tentative call with Vince for late afternoon, or early evening, to see where we were at with the hotel acquisition. I laced my fingers with Adeline's, needing the reassurance of her touch after Tommy had almost taken her away. The emotions from that incident, merging with the vision I'd had, were an explosive mix I couldn't shake.

The elevator dinged, and we exited to our suite. After dropping off the bags and a quick kiss, I headed out with the intent to see Adeline next in the rooms that functioned as our offices. There were things I had to handle—specifically, Celia.

"Mr. Crenshaw," Steve flagged me down when I stepped off the elevator onto the second floor.

Sawdust coated his pants. He stood with arms full of paint cans, and a grim set to his mouth. "I hate to be the one to tell you this, but I don't want what happened to reflect badly on Delilah. She's a hard worker and gets along with my guys and her team. Or most of them."

"What's the problem then?"

"The Tuscan tiles Delilah ordered were sent back."

Banked anger simmered. "Let me guess, Celia had a hand in that?"

Steve nodded. "One of my guys saw her intercept the delivery."

"Thanks, Steve." I clapped him on the shoulder. "I'll handle it."

I found both women in one of the second-floor guest rooms. Ignoring Delilah and the other two members of the design team who were busy replicating the missing, or torn, sections of nineteenth-century wallpaper with careful application of paint. I walked straight to Celia. She was off to the side of the room, flipping through one of the sample books for the project.

"A word?" The vein in my neck pulsed as her expression went from indifferent to calculating when she zeroed in on me. I waved my hand toward the doorway. We needed to have this conversation where it wasn't overheard.

As she passed, her arm brushed against me, and my fury over what she'd done went up another notch. Following behind her, I took in her sleek hair, designer clothes, and ridiculous heels. It was so obvious she wasn't here to get any actual work completed. The rest of the team wore jeans and shirts with paint splatters on them from their efforts in replicating the wallpaper.

Once we were in the empty guest room, I shut the door with a resounding click. I turned to face her. She was too close. When she lifted a palm to rest it on my chest, I moved away, unable to stop my anger from erupting.

"Get your things and get out of my hotel. You no longer work for Stone Enterprises."

Other than the slight flair to her pupils, she appeared unaffected. "You don't mean that." She spoke as if she was chastising a small child. "We both know Adeline isn't good enough for you. Not to mention she's engaged to that football player."

I refused to involve myself in the bullshit she was spewing. It was never about family standing to me, nor would it ever be. "You put one of my employees at risk with your latest stunt."

"Hardly." She lifted a slim shoulder and let it fall.

"He tried to take her away against her will! That's harm. Not to mention you disclosed private company information. We were in a meeting at the time, which you knew."

"Nothing was confidential."

"How did you know about it?"

She waved her hand, virtually dismissing my question.

"Celia," I growled.

"I have access to her calendar."

"That's login and password protected."

She shrugged. "Adeline had the email open with all the information for everyone to see. None of that will matter since she's leaving. And I'm sure the happy couple will iron their misunderstanding out."

"That isn't happening."

"They're much more suited for one another with their backgrounds." That calculating gleam intensified. "As for no longer working here, if you're suggesting we move our relationship to the next level and my employment is a problem, I agree."

"That's not—" I growled.

"—There is a fundraiser coming up that will be important for us to attend. I'll accept the invitation on our behalf."

"I've informed your uncle you no longer work here. You're fired, Celia."

She crossed her arms over her chest, something I knew she rarely did, as it was too visually confrontational. I didn't have the patience for this.

"I'm not going anywhere, Stone. You promised me we'd end up together, that we were perfect for each other."

Goddamn it. "No, Celia. I did not. We had one, maybe two dates when we were younger, both of which my mother twisted my arm into. I never gave you the idea we would get married."

"Our mothers—"

"—are friends. I have no control over their gossiping about what they hoped would happen. And I never gave you the impression anything further would come of us attending the obligated family functions."

Yanking open the doors, I left her standing there. If I'd stayed and tried to reason with her, I wasn't sure I could keep my voice to a reasonable level or stop myself from shaking some sense into her to in an attempt dislodge her particular brand of crazy.

I ran my fingers through my hair, tugging on the strands before releasing them. With hurried steps, I found Steve, the rest of the construction and design crew, and briefed them that Celia was no longer employed here. A quick stop to security, and they were aware and in search of her to ensure she left the premises.

One headache gone, I hoped. With long strides, I made my way back to the penthouse. There were things I had to straighten out with Adeline—mainly, our future.

***

Adeline

STONE BURST THROUGH THE DOOR TO OUR SUITE WITH HAIR that looked as if he'd dragged his fingers through it several times. "Everything okay?" By the expression on his face, it wasn't. Celia must have put up a fight.

"Yes." He loosened his tie. "I fired her. You need to change your password. That's how she had access to my calendar. Security is making sure she leaves the premises. Her uncle has another position lined up for her as a fashion design assistant in the States. She won't bother us any longer." Dropping onto the settee next to me, he took my hands in his. "We need to discuss your future and our fake engagement."

"Okay." My spine stiffened, and I braced myself for the impact his serious demeanor indicated.

"I have a confession to make. I wasn't completely honest with you when I forced your hand regarding the fake fiancée contract."

"Hmm."

His thumb rubbed back and forth across the back of my hand, and I took comfort from that simple gesture while I waited for the bomb to drop.

"I know we haven't met before, but when we first ran into one another, I was drawn to you. There was this deep sense of familiarity, and I didn't want to let you go. Ever since I moved into this hotel, I've been having odd dreams that reflect the nineteenth century, and you're in them. Well, not exactly you, but a woman who bares a similar resemblance. I was shocked when you bumped into me the evening you arrived here and how much I was drawn to you."

"To me or a woman that lives in your dreams?"

"No. Not her. It's all you. I only shared that so you would understand that there's something else here. It's as if I already knew you when we first met."

"Okay…" Even though I understood what he was talking

about, I didn't want to make any rash assumptions to where he was going with this discussion. "So, our fake engagement wasn't to help seal the deal with the Venice hotel?"

His lips curved into that wolfish grin I loved. "Oh, that was necessary, but my driving emotion behind it was to keep you close."

"I see. And now?"

"Now, I want to make it real."

My hand jerked in his. "That seems a little premature."

He shrugged. "I always put a hundred percent effort in going after what I want."

I raised my eyebrows at him and tried to slow my racing heart. I needed to tell him about the letters I'd found in Cristiano's room. "I didn't quite recognize you as you did with me, not right away, but a part of me had when we touched." Our first touch had felt like a live wire in my hand. I still remembered the sensation and the vision I'd had. And with that thought, I wanted to share the notes with him. "I stumbled across something in the basement you should see."

Stone stiffened at the mention of the lower level. I tugged my hand free and went to retrieve the cigar box from my bedroom. With care, I brought it back to the settee we were sitting on together, placing the antique box on the coffee table. "I found this under the floorboards in one of the rooms. I think this will explain what we're experiencing."

Most of the color leached from his face, and I moved closer to him. "Do you recognize it?" I held my breath as he brushed his hand over the edge of the wood, the smallest nod letting me know I wasn't alone in the visions I'd had.

"How did you—"

"—I tripped."

His laugh filled the room, lightening the seriousness of our discussion. "Have you read these already?"

Heat rushed up to my neck and infused my cheeks. "Not

all of them." There were only a handful of notes. I handed him the stack and leaned close so I could read them again too.

In a flowing script, the first was from Cristiano, waxing on about Francesca's beauty. He'd asked her to meet him in the courtyard at midnight. The next was her response, a simple acceptance of the date.

It wasn't until the last letter that tears flowed unchecked down my face. Francesca's mother had spotted them one evening with their heads bent toward one another. She'd put an end to the possibility of their young love, informing her that they would be leaving in the morning. Francesca was saying goodbye.

Cristiano, my love,

My hand shakes from the devastating news I must share with you. Madre spied us in the gardens, witnessing our kiss. She and Padre were enraged, and after hours of pleading, I convinced them not to file a complaint against you or your padre. In their acquiescence, they posed a stipulation—I must leave with them at once come first light.

My heart breaks at the thought of parting from you, but it is the only way I can ensure your family's livelihood will not be affected. My love for you is greater than any fleeting thought to my happiness.

God willing, we will have a moment alone before they take me away from Verona, and you.

Yours through all time,

Francesca

I slipped my arm through the crook of Stone's as we strolled along the sidewalk, heading toward Juliet's Wall. The sun climbed the sky as we neared the busy square, and I imagined how it had looked back in the nineteenth century. The square's ambiance tricked time and space, and it was easy to imagine we were indeed in the past where our star-crossed muses had been.

The space was thick with emotion, and it was impossible not to get caught up in it. Hope, lovers reunited, unfulfilled, and heartbreak. But the promise of possibility amplified what we were feeling, and I leaned in to Stone's side, needing the connection as we strolled through the square.

Vines climbed the castle's walls, and gothic architecture decorated the palace. The fragrant air wrapped around us as a lover's arms would. Romance permeated the space. As we rounded a corner, I glimpsed Juliet's statue.

"Isn't the myth that if you rub the statue's right breast, you'll have luck?"

Stone nodded then flashed me that sexy crooked grin. "We'll make our own luck." He pointed to a section of the famous wall that was covered in notes and ink. We walked along the historical monument to the space he'd indicated, weaving in and out of the crowd until we neared the edge. We both stopped, and I fought the urge to look over my shoulder to ensure no one watched us. The area of brick he pointed to was what I'd seen in one of my visions. "Let's start looking over there."

"I'm nervous." My entire body vibrated with anticipation. This was where Cristiano and his love had arranged secret meetings and planned for their future until they were torn apart by family and social status.

"The balcony—" Stone pointed to the small outdoor space that symbolized where Juliet would have stood. "Wasn't added until the twentieth century."

"So our star-crossed lovers wouldn't have seen it."

"No." With a gentle tug, he guided us closer to the corner of the wall, the general area where Cristiano secreted away his letters for Francesca.

My fingers trailed along the bricks, tracing a myriad of graffiti that lamented about love, hope, and promises made. The closer we got to the section that held their hiding place, the more my mind tugged. I wanted to follow the hazy pictures that danced on the edges of consciousness.

"Adeline."

Stone had stopped. His deep baritone pulled me from the inner shadows of my mind and back to the brightly lit present. He played with the engagement ring on my finger. "There was a reason I gave you this specific piece of jewelry. It was meant to be yours."

My breath caught at the sincerity in his voice, and I glanced at the sparkling heirloom ring that felt right on my finger. Then he lowered himself to one knee and took my left hand in his.

"I don't believe it's a coincidence we collided your first

night in Verona. You've haunted my dreams and every waking moment since I set foot here. Let's change history. Will you be my wife, for real this time?"

I, too, felt the same connection, and joy shot through me at his proposal. At that moment, everything felt right, and I leapt into his arms. Clinging to his neck, I laughed. "Yes." I didn't care that we'd only known one another for a short time. That was not how it seemed. It was as if we'd spent lifetimes together, and when we were by each other's side, the world aligned perfectly. There was no one else I'd rather be with.

Stone stood with me pressed tightly to him. As his head tilted toward me, I lifted to my toes. His lips teased mine open. I threaded my fingers through his thick hair, urging him impossibly closer. As he explored my mouth, I lost myself in the kiss. Tingles spread over every inch of my body. My head spun from desire, and our surroundings faded.

He drew back from my lips, creating a small amount of space between us. I felt the loss instantly and shivered. The noise of so many people surrounding us filtered in, and I forced myself down from my toes and took a small step back. His arms stayed at my waist, fingers spread, anchoring me so I couldn't go far. Not that I would. I was more than fine with our close proximity to one another. I played with the ends of his hair at the nape of his neck while emotions swirled in his eyes like a stormy sky.

"What do you remember?"

I sucked in a breath. We'd talked about the things we'd seen, but there was so much more. "Do you think they're us? Or we're them?"

He moved his head in a barely noticeable left-to-right motion. "I can't wrap my brain around that. But it would explain a lot: the undeniable force that propelled me to buy the hotel, the dreams, the feelings of loss, of despair originating from the basement." His fingers caressed my cheek. "You."

If there was even a tiny part of me that was holding back from loving him, it no longer existed. I fell all the way.

"It doesn't matter to me." His hand cupped the side of my face. "I think the history of the hotel, the tragedy of their story, is what influenced us. Even the possibility that they brought us here for reasons we may never fully understand."

My eyes misted at the thought of Cristiano and Francesca's restless spirits. Could our actions bring them together in some way? "Maybe they wanted someone like them to have a happy ever after." There was no doubt that their souls were unsettled with how things had ended. Why else would we have been so affected staying there? Dreams and visions hadn't plagued us in Venice or anywhere else for that matter. But from the conversations Stone and I had, we had both been drawn to the hotel in Verona for one reason or another. "I hope we were able to help them attain peace."

I nibbled on my kiss-swollen lip, an idea forming that I thought would satisfy the ghosts of Francesca and Cristiano, as well as lift the residue of unhappiness and despair Stone sensed clinging to the walls, particularly the basement.

With reluctance, we drew apart. It was time. As we stepped to the wall, our hands clasped. Miraculously, the area we'd wanted to view was devoid of the throng of people present everywhere else in the square.

"That's the one." Stone nodded at a brick with a vein of off-white bisecting its surface.

I ran my fingers across it, and then he wiggled it until it came loose. "Oh." There was a piece of folded paper pushed against the back where the brick had been. After I removed it, a flash of silver drew my attention. Pinching a delicate chain, I removed a necklace with a pendant that dangled.

"It's the same as mine!" My fingers grazed the pendant of Saint Valentine I wore around my neck. Saint Valentine was known as the patron saint of lovers.

"I saw it in my dreams," Stone said as he returned the stone to its rightful place in the wall. "Cristiano gave it to Francesca. That's why I was surprised you wore the same one. It makes sense that you were drawn to it."

Our gazes caught and held. Everything in me settled as he slipped his arm around my waist, and we began our walk back to the hotel. We were bringing that last part of them home.

ADELINE

Almost a month had passed, and a hint of chilly weather seeped into the air as dusk embraced Verona. Fall was upon us, and the changing colors blanketed the countryside. I didn't have a favorite season in Italy yet. But I had a lifetime to figure it out.

Stone slept better at night now, so long as I was in the same bed as he was. We'd extended our stay to see the hotel to completion, and then Tiffany would manage it part-time, in addition to hiring any staff she needed.

Venice would be our next adventure, but Stone was no longer in such a hurry. He recognized a kindred soul in Vince and had proposed a collaboration so that he and his wife, Margaret, maintained partial ownership of their life-long dream.

They went a step further and reached out to Nick Reynolds, the hotelier they had discussed when we were all out to dinner one night, to begin a partnership with his financially compromised Grande Victorian Hotel, utilizing my ideas. As for my job, it was everything I had ever wanted and more. Stone and I worked as a team as we expanded and fortified our empire.

The dreams and visions had tapered off when we'd brought the necklace and letter Cristiano had written to Francesca back to the hotel, as if reuniting pieces of their past offered a semblance of closure, a balm of sorts to the pain of their separation.

I waited in Cristiano's room for Stone to come down to the lower level, the picture frame heavy in my hands. This wasn't the first time Stone had ventured into the basement since Delilah had come up with her genius plan. The crushing sense of loss no longer plagued him.

Delilah's design had created a space where the ambiance was that of another world. Hints of simple living, like the small kitchenette at the bottom, and off to the side, of the narrow stairs, giving homage to a time past. It was charming and updated in a way that the modern conveniences were concealed so as not to take away from the theme. In keeping with Cristiano and Francesca's time period, we furnished it with high-end eighteen-century style furniture and murals. The linens were of the finest quality and offered an oasis of luxury, a haven beneath the decadence a floor above. To rent the lower level delivered the experience of another life, a world away from civilization.

It was an escape.

It was our gift to Cristiano and Francesca's memories. A complete apartment with all the trimmings a wealthy station in life would have offered. Including period clothing our guests could choose from when we held monthly historical balls or murder mystery games.

During the lower level renovation, we'd discovered a forgotten box that contained pictures of the staff and a few of the guests that had stayed at the hotel. I'd done my research and learned Cristiano had died from a lung infection a few years after Francesca had drowned. Their lives, and their romance, were cut tragically short.

With everything we had done, the conversation I'd had with the psychic nagged in the back of my mind. She'd told me my mom had named me after a relative lost at sea. I'd contacted Tommy and had him go to the storage locker where I'd left some things from my parent's house. He'd found what I was looking for and sent it through the mail—a notebook of Mom's. When I received it, I had my answer. Within the handwritten pages, she had documented our family tree. Francesca's middle name was Adeline.

There were times we could feel Cristiano and Francesca's essence, their fated love. But the despair and tragedy no longer pierced our souls, as we believed they'd found their peace and their way back to one another.

"There you are." Stone came up behind me, his hands resting on my hips.

I leaned against his chest, and a shiver coursed over my body as I admired my handiwork of the mounted letter we'd recovered from Juliet's Wall within the frame. "Are you ready to do this?"

He bent to my ear and murmured, "Always."

My eyelids grew heavy, and I wanted him to turn me in his arms and kiss me senseless. A soft sigh whispered through the room, and a different kind of chill chased the one of desire away.

I drew away from Stone. "Did you hear that?"

His gaze was smoky, full of promise, and his tempting lips curved into a wicked half grin. "Mm-hm."

"That wasn't me." I waited a second until the desire lifted from his features as well. "Let's get this hung." This wasn't the time for us. It was for them.

Delilah had already installed the hanging system. All we needed to do was put the framed shadow box on it, together.

Stone grasped one side of the frame, and I held onto the other. We placed it on the hook then stepped back to admire the contents.

Behind the protected glass was the last letter from Cristiano to Francesca, alongside the Saint Valentine pendant necklace that he'd given her to symbolize their destiny. I scanned over his flowy, inked words. Unable to help myself, I reread them.

My dearest Francesca,

Not a day goes by that I don't long to hear your laughter, feel the touch of your hand in mine, or to brush your moon-spun hair behind the delicate shell of your ear and whisper to you how loved you are.

As the days turn to weeks and then to months, my despair over how I'll gain my fortune and win your hand becomes a greater challenge. I promise you this, Francesca, I will never erase you from my heart. You are always in my mind, no matter what circumstance has torn us apart. Somehow, someday, we will be together again.

All my love,

Cristiano

"Do you think they've found each other?" His letter was dated soon after he fell ill. Somehow, he must have had a sense that there was a chance he wouldn't survive. My eyes misted at the tragedy of their lives. Based on the letter, Cristiano never knew Francesca hadn't made it to her destination, that the ship she was on had sunk. Their story broke my heart.

"I do." Stone's arm around my waist held me tight to his side. He turned us to face the opposite wall. "The mural of them is…"

"Yeah," I said on a sigh. We'd described them in greater detail to an artist we had commissioned, in addition to sharing the pictures we'd found and had framed in the open area of the basement. The mural was of Francesca leaning against Cristiano, his hands wrapped around her waist as we were doing now. One look at their expressions, and their love for one another was a tangible thing. The artist had made them lifelike for others; for us, they already were.

A sense of contentment, romance, and fate filled the room. After the mural's paint was dry, their presence had saturated the room so much so that we'd realized there would be another purpose within these four walls.

We'd turned it into a haven for the star-crossed lovers, as well as a space to read in, or of reflection for our guests that rented the lower level. Within the room were two ornate chaise lounges, a bookcase filled with rare books, a softly glowing chandelier, and shadow box tables that contained jewelry, ledgers, and various photographs from the hotel during that time period.

In another portion of the basement, we'd knocked down walls and turned a few of the rooms into one large, luxurious bedroom, complete with an en suite bathroom.

Those weren't the only changes we had made. We'd made the hotel experience center around Cristiano and Francesca's love story. Each note was framed and placed in a themed room. We then offered suggestions of which room guests should stay in next upon their return so they could get the full story of their love affair in chronological order. After finding a cache of nineteenth-century photos of the hotel, it's guests and staff, we used them to enhance the ambiance and mystery of the hotel.

Stone slipped his arms from around my waist and threaded our fingers together. Everything felt right, complete, and we shared a satisfied yet nostalgic smile.

"Let's go to the courtyard." Stone tugged my hand, and I followed him up the stairs and outside. A plaque and bench commemorated Cristiano and Francesca's clandestine meetings under the witness of the stars and moon. To the side of their love seat glider was a large outdoor tent with a king-sized mattress and necessities that gave a sort of glamping experience for guests to reserve—built on a deck with two comfortable chairs under a small overhang from the tent. A stone inlay surrounded the outdoor room, expanding to a winding trail where they could sit around a fire pit, or dine under the stars at a handcrafted wood table beneath a pergola. At night, lanterns glowed, and the magic of the experience was in full bloom. Specified themes and activities were available to choose from by the guests, prior to their reservation. It was a slice of heaven that was already booked up months in advance when our website went live.

"I love it here." I couldn't help the sigh from escaping my lips—so much romance. I hoped Stone would want to visit often, in between our adventures. After we'd found Cristiano's letter and brought it home, things had changed. Stone was in better spirits, no longer haunted by Cristiano's pining and feelings of despair. "You're not having any more dreams?"

"No, not anymore." He tucked a piece of my hair behind my ear and brushed a kiss across my lips. "We did what needed to be done here. The hotel will be a success, and we'll leave tomorrow for our next business venture."

Venice. I smiled and pressed closer to him, my engagement ring sparkling in the light. Who would have thought that psychic my best friend Eileen had hired would be right? My destiny was in Italy. "I can't wait." With Stone by my side, I was excited for our next adventure. "Let's go for a walk to Juliet's Wall."

The End

Continue reading more of Amy's books with, Moonlit Mirage, or for edge-of-your-seat action, check out Broken Circle, book one in the Gray Ghost romantic suspense thriller series.

https://amymckinleyauthor.com/moonlit-destination-series/
https://amymckinleyauthor.com/gray-ghost-series/

Keep up with Amy's releases by joining her newsletter: http://eepurl.com/dEBqJn

---

If you enjoyed reading FAKE FIANCÉ as much as I did writing it, I hope you'll consider leaving a review.

ACKNOWLEDGMENTS

I have a confession to make—this was supposed to be an easy project that consumed maybe two weeks of writing. It wasn't. And I have to thank Maryellen Newton for all her encouragement to stay in my chair and get the story written. It's a different story than what I'm used to writing, minus the edge of your seat action and adventure. Stone and Adeline were enticing and hooked me as their story unfolded, and I hope you enjoyed them as well.

Each book is a unique journey, and I am so grateful to all those with me along the way.

To my family for their encouragement, support, and unwavering belief.

To my critique partners Emily Albright and Kristin Kisska—talented authors whose insight and friendships are so valued. Brainstorming sessions are so much fun with them. To Maria Vickers, who provided incredible feedback in her beta read.

To Taylor Anhalt, my brilliant and talented editor who finds time to fit me in regardless of how busy she is. Due to what's happening in the world this year (2020), we couldn't spend hours at Panera. I'm looking forward to everything opening in the not too distant future and logging more coffee induced writing time with her there.

This book was first published in Sinful Secrets (A Contemporary Romance Box Set). There, I got to work with some incredible authors and enjoyed the months we spent together promoting and working together. All the proceeds were donated to the leading charity fighting hunger in America. It was a worthy cause, and I thank everyone who purchased the set and helped feed those who needed assistance during this crazy pandemic.

USA Today bestselling author Rachel Rawlings helped me with some of the box set tasks, and we came to be great friends during that time. I am very grateful for her support, encouragement, and friendship.

T.E. Black Designs, who did the cover design Each project exceeds my expectations.

Last but certainly not least, a special thanks to Colleen Noyes, the owner of Itsy Bitsy Book Bits, with her unfailing encouragement and support. Her staff and readers are wonderful and dedicated and so very appreciated.

A huge thank you to all the bloggers and readers who have encouraged and helped me along the way, and who continue to make my dream a reality.

Thank you.

ABOUT THE AUTHOR

 **Amy McKinley** is the *USA Today* Bestselling author of the romantic suspense thriller Gray Ghost Novels, Moonlit Destination series, Deadly Isles Special Ops, Five Fates paranormal romance series, and several stand-alone titles. Her edge-of-your-seat books are filled with surprising twists and just the right amount of heat and danger. She lives in Illinois with her husband, two daughters, two sons, and three mischievous cats.

You can find her at:
www.AmyMcKinley.com

facebook.com/amymckinleyauthor
twitter.com/AmyMcKinley7
instagram.com/amymckinleyauthor
bookbub.com/profile/amy-mckinley

Hidden
Taken

Hidden
Taken